George Quayle Cannon

The Life of Nephi, the Son of Lehi

Who emigrated from Jerusalem, in Judea, to the land which is now known
as South America, about six centuries before the coming of the Savior

George Quayle Cannon

The Life of Nephi, the Son of Lehi
Who emigrated from Jerusalem, in Judea, to the land which is now known as South America, about six centuries before the coming of the Savior

ISBN/EAN: 9783337315207

Printed in Europe, USA, Canada, Australia, Japan

Cover: Foto ©Raphael Reischuk / pixelio.de

More available books at **www.hansebooks.com**

THE SON OF LEHI,

Who Emigrated from Jerusalem, in Judea, to the Land
which is now known as South America, about
Six Centuries Before the Coming
of the Savior.

• ✦ •

NINTH BOOK OF THE

FAITH-PROMOTING SERIES.

————•▶►◀•————

BY GEORGE Q. CANNON,

*Of the First Presidency of the Church of Jesus Christ of
Latter-day Saints.*

SALT LAKE CITY, UTAH:

Published by the Juvenile Instructor Office.

1888.

PREFACE.

SOME years since the desire took possession of me to write the life of Nephi, the son of Lehi, and, as time and opportunity should permit, the lives of other prominent men of his race of whom we have an account in the Book of Mormon, so as to form a series of biographies for the perusal of the young. My aim was to make the children of our Church familiar with the events described in the Book of Mormon, and with some of the prominent men of that mighty people of which Nephi was one of the greatest progenitors. Various causes—the principal one of which has been the pressure of other and more exacting labors—have prevented me from carrying my design into execution until the present time. I have felt that, as I owed so much of my own success in life to the important and interesting lessons contained in that precious record, it was a duty incumbent upon me to do all in my power to have it read and appreciated as widely as possible by every member of our Church, but especially by the rising generation.

The age in which we live is one of doubt and unbelief. Skepticism is spreading. All faith in divine things, as taught by the ancient servants of God, is being unsettled. Man's reason is being extolled as a higher standard than God's revelations. The personality of God, the origin of man and his fall, the atonement of the Savior the places of reward and punishment, known as heaven and hell, and the existence of a personal devil, are all questioned, and, by many members of religious sects denied. The Bible is no longer accepted as a reliable standard, only so far as its teachings may agree with the new and fashionable views entertained respecting religion and science.

Fortunately for us, we are in a position to stem and turn this tide of infidelity, so that it shall not overwhelm our young people. We are not dependent upon the Bible alone for our knowledge concerning these grand, cardinal truths over which the world is stumbling and debating. We have other records —among the most important of which is the Book of Mormon —which corroborate and furnish ample proofs of their heavenly origin. We have the teachings and knowledge of men living in lands far apart and of races widely separated; and they agree in their testimonies, and sustain the divinity of the truths which are taught by the Son of God Himself, and by His inspired servants.

The Prophet Nephi, whose life we here present, was one of the greatest and most advanced of these teachers of heavenly truths. There have been but few men, so far as we know, who comprehended, and spoke, and wrote about them as plainly as did he. He had a personal knowledge of the doctrines, principles and facts respecting which men now dispute. He has written fully upon them. His testimony, therefore, is worth more to the world than any number of men's opinions and theories. And, best of all, it carries within itself the highest evidence of its truth. This is characteristic of his writings, and of all the writings in the Book of Mormon. To every humble, prayerful soul the perusal of that book is a solace. It produces peace and joy, and brings the clear conviction that it is God's word. No arguments are required to prove this. Men have assailed and denounced it; but the indisputable truth still remains that, when read with a meek spirit and a prayerful heart, the testimony of its divine origin descends like refreshing dew from heaven, upon the reader, and he knows, by the Spirit and power of God, that it is His word.

That THE LIFE OF NEPHI may have the effect to increase faith, and stimulate inquiry and the more careful perusal of the divine records which the Lord has given to us, is the most earnest desire of   THE AUTHOR.

CONTENTS.

CHAPTER XIII.

CHAPTER XIV.

CHAPTER XV.

CHAPTER XIX.

CHAPTER XX.

CHAPTER XXI.

THE LIFE OF NEPHI.

CHAPTER I.

OF all the lives which have come down to us in the ancient
records, there is, probably, not one, excepting our Savior's,
which can be studied with more profit than that of Nephi, the
son of Lehi. The influence which he exerted over his associates was most wonderful; but it did not end there. We think
we do not overrate it when we say that no man of the nation of
which he was the founder did so much as he towards giving
shape to the methods of government, to the forms of worship
and to the mode of life which prevailed for about a thousand
years among that people. He was to them what Moses was to
the children of Israel, and though the Nephite nation was prolific in great men, there was not one, it seems to us, who
exceeded, if indeed he came up in every particular to, the full
measure of his greatness. So far as the record of his life has
come down to us, it presents the picture of a man of such per-
fections as has rarely been seen on earth. He does not leave us
in doubt as to why this was the case. The success which
attended all his undertakings he claimed no credit for. At no
time does he indulge in self-glorification; but in all that he says
the disposition to give God the glory is very apparent. He
gives him the glory for it all. To this, more than any other
cause, do we attribute the prosperity which attended him
through life. and which made him the truly great man that he

was. Speaking of himself, he says that he had been highly
favored of the Lord in all his days.

Nephi, the son of Lehi, was born at Jerusalem. The exact
year of his birth is not given; but we can form a very good idea
of the time from what he says respecting himself. His father,
Lehi, and family left Jerusalem six hundred years before the
coming of the Savior. Nephi, alluding to himself soon after
this, while they were in the wilderness, describes himself as
"exceeding young, nevertheless large in stature." The record
leads us to the conclusion that he was a man in size, though a
boy in years—probably not more than fifteen years old. From
the language of his brother Jacob in the beginning of his book
we infer that Nephi did not live long after the year fifty-five of
their exodus from Jerusalem. Jacob says, "he began to be
old." He was doubtless at least seventy years old at that time.
We judge, therefore, that he was born not far from the year
615 B. C. This would be in the reign of Josiah, the father of
Zedekiah, and whose reign closed between eleven and twelve
years before the latter was put upon the throne of Judah by
the conqueror, Nebuchadnezzar, king of Babylon.

We are not told as to how his childhood was spent. It is
evident, however, that his father was in affluent circumstances;
for besides his house and land, he had gold, silver and other
precious things in abundance; in fact, so much of this kind of
personal property did he have, that upon one occasion, it was
coveted, as we shall see as we proceed with his history, and was
the cause of an attempt to kill Nephi and his three older brothers.
Nephi, himself, says he was "born of goodly parents," and he
doubtless received an education suitable to his station; he "was
taught somewhat in all the learning" of his father.

Lehi had always lived at Jerusalem. He was a descendant of
Manasseh, the oldest son of Joseph, who was sold by his brothers. He must have witnessed stirring times in his native
city; for though he doubtless shared in the peace and prosperity which prevailed during the long and successful reign of the
faithful king, Josiah, he saw no less than four kings on the
throne of Judah in the brief space of eleven or twelve years.
King Josiah was succeeded by his son Jehoahaz, whose reign
of three months was brought to a close by the king of Egypt

carrying him to Egypt and laying the land of Judah under tribute and making Jehoiakim, his brother, king in his stead. Jehoiakim reigned eleven years, and in the first part of his reign was a tributary to the king of Egypt, who had put him on the throne. Afterwards he fell into the power of Nebuchadnezzar, the king of Babylon, and for three years he acknowledged him as his superior; then he rebelled. But there was a curse upon him and his family, because of his wickedness; the Lord had taken their strength from them; they could not break the yoke of the foe which was raised up against them. Josephus informs us that:

"The king of Babylon made an expedition against Jerusalem and was received by the king Jehoiakim into the city. But he slew such as were of the flower of their age and such as were of the greatest dignity, together with their king Jehoiakim, whom he commanded to be thrown before the wall without any burial."

Jehoiakim was succeeded by his son Jehoiachin, whose inglorious reign of a little over three months, was terminated by the siege of Jerusalem by Nebuchadnezzar, and his marching out of the city and surrendering himself, his wives, his mother, his princes and officers to that king. He and they were all carried prisoners to Babylon. The king of Babylon also took as prisoners upwards of ten thousand of the nobility and leading men of the land, among whom was the prophet Ezekiel. Nebuchadnezzar then made Zedekiah, the uncle of the last king, and brother of his father, king of Judah.

It was in the midst of scenes like these that Nephi's childhood was spent. His father must have been familiar with the predictions of the Prophet Jeremiah, who for upwards of thirty years before Lehi and family left Jerusalem, had been declaring the word of the Lord unto the people. It is more than likely that he knew him personally. At the time of Nephi's last visit to Jerusalem the Prophet Jeremiah was in prison. There were other prophets also, whom Lehi either knew personally, or, at least, was acquainted with their predictions. Nephi, as a child, was trained in the knowledge of the prophecies. This is apparent in his teachings. He quotes the words of three prophets, of whose predictions we have no record

—Zenock, Neum and Zenos—except the quotations from them which appear in the Book of Mormon. Their predictions and the predictions of another prophet—of which none have yet come to us—Ezais by name, as well as those of Moses, Joseph, Isaiah, and all the prophets from the beginning down to his own day, they brought with them upon plates of brass to this land. Nephi, in speaking of the prophecies of Isaiah, from which he quoted largely, says that the Jews understood the things of the prophets spoken unto them as no other people not taught after their manner could. That he was trained in these things at Jerusalem is easily perceived from what he says; for he understood their style, and their predictions were plain to him. This was an advantage to him afterwards in teaching his people.

CHAPTER II.

TRUE AND FALSE PROPHETS—LEHI'S VISION—HE WARNS THE PEOPLE—THEY PERSECUTE AND TRY TO KILL HIM—COM-MANDED IN A DREAM TO TAKE HIS FAMILY INTO THE WIL-DERNESS—CAME TO RED SEA—CAMPED NEAR IT—BUILT AN ALTAR AND MADE OFFERING TO THE LORD—LAMAN AND LEMUEL.—THEIR UNBELIEF—SHAKEN AND CON-FOUNDED BEFORE THEIR FATHER.

IN the beginning of the first year of Zedekiah's reign there were many prophets in Jerusalem. The events connected with the recent siege of that city were of such a character as to arouse thought and prompt men who feared God to feel after Him. We learn from another source than Nephi's record that there were many false prophets at those times who misled the people and were the means of causing them to harden their hearts against the truth. The prophets of God told the people of Jeru-salem they must repent, or that great city must be destroyed. These predictions had their proper effect upon Lehi. He undoubtedly believed them, and he went out and called upon the Lord with all his heart in behalf of his people. While praying there came a pillar of fire and rested upon a rock before him. We are told by Nephi that he saw and heard much, which caused him to quake and tremble exceedingly. After this he returned to his house, and being overcome by the Spirit and the things which he had seen he was carried away in a vision. He saw the heavens open, and he thought he saw God sitting upon a throne, surrounded by numberless concourses of angels in the attitude of singing and praising Him. He saw one descending out of heaven, whose lustre was above that of the sun at noon day. He was followed by twelve others, whose brightness exceeded that of the stars. They all came down and went forth upon the face of the earth. The first, however, came and stood before Lehi and gave him a book, and told him to read. As he read he was filled with the Spirit of God. And he read, "Wo, wo unto Jerusalem; for I have seen thy abominations." He read many things concerning Jerusalem, that it should be destroyed, and that many of its inhabitants should perish by the sword, and that many should be carried away captive into Babylon. He read and saw many marvelous things, which caused him to praise the Lord in the following language: "Great and marvelous are thy works, O Lord God Almighty! Thy throne is high in the heavens and thy power and goodness, and mercy are over all the inhabitants of the earth; and because thou are merciful, thou will not suffer those who come unto thee that they shall perish!" The soul of Lehi rejoiced and his whole heart was filled, because of the things which the Lord had shown him.

This is the feeling which every one has to whom the Lord reveals Himself as He did to Lehi. There is a pure and heavenly joy rests upon him that language cannot describe or express, and in the presence of which the afflictions which he has to endure, because of the persecutions of men, appear trifling and are easily borne. Having had these visions Lehi could not rest without warning his neighbors and the people of the city. He described to them their wickedness and abominations, and testified that the things which he had seen and heard, and also that which he had read in the book, manifested plainly of the coming of a Messiah and also the redemption of the world. To tell wicked people of their sins and of the destruction of their government or city makes them angry. It wounds their self-love; it insults their personal and national pride, and it scarcely ever fails to arouse their hatred. There was an exception to this which occurs to us. Upon one occasion the wickedness of the people of Nineveh, the Lord said, had come up to Him. He sent the Prophet Jonah to warn them, and they believed God; and from the king on his throne to the lowest in the city, including all their animals, they wore sackcloth, and fasted. They turned every one from his evil way, and from the violence that was in his hands, and cried mightily unto the Lord. Their repentance was pleasing unto the Lord, and He turned from them the judgment he had threatened. Unfortunately for the people of Jerusalem, they did not have that spirit. Their hearts were hard. They would not believe Lehi; but they mocked him, grew angry with him, just as they had with other prophets before him whom they had cast out, stoned and slain, and they tried to kill him. Had he remained among them, and continued his prophesying, they doubtless would have killed him. But the Lord had chosen him for another work. and he escaped from their plots. The Lord spoke unto him in a dream, and after blessing him for what he had done, in faithfully declaring unto the Jews that which He had commanded him—for doing which they had sought to take his life —He commanded him that he should take his family and depart into the wilderness.

Lehi's family consisted at that time of his wife Sariah and four sons—Laman, Lemuel, Sam and Nephi—that we know of. Nephi, some years after this (*II. Nephi viii.*, 6) speaks of his sisters. He does not mention them as members of the family at the time of leaving Jerusalem, and we are left to conjecture whether they were born before leaving Jerusalem or afterwards.

Lehi did not hesitate about obeying the commandment. It was probably a matter of life or death with him. He had either to leave, or be killed if he continued to prophesy. Hence it was that among his descendants the expression was used, "Our father, Lehi, was driven out of Jerusalem." (*Helaman viii.*, 22.) Nephi himself, in speaking of the people of that city said: "They have driven him out of the land." Lehi did not load himself down with his gold and silver and other valuables these he left with his house and land. He took his family, his provisions and tents, and started. After traveling in the wilderness he came to the Red Sea, and he continued his journey near its borders. He soon reached a valley by the side and near the mouth of a river, which emptied into the Red Sea. Here he pitched his tent, and the family remained encamped sometime. He built at this place an altar of stones and made an offering unto the Lord and gave Him thanks. The river he called Laman, the name of his oldest son; the valley he called Lemuel, the name of his second son. Up to this point we are told nothing of the character of Lehi's family. But Nephi tells us that after stopping at this river and in this valley and giving to them these names, his father took occasion to say to Laman:

"O that thou mightest be like unto this river, continually running into the fountain of all righteousness."

And to say to Lemuel:

"O that thou mightest be like unto this valley, firm and steadfast, and immoveable in keeping the commandments of the Lord."

Nephi gives the reasons why his father talked in this way to his two oldest sons. They were young men who had no faith in the things which their father had taught. They had the same spirit of unbelief which the Jews had who sought to kill their father. They called him a visionary man, and they murmured against him because he had taken them away from Jerusalem, from the land of their inheritance, and their gold and silver and other precious things and led them into the wilderness. They did not believe that Jerusalem could be destroyed as the prophets had predicted. Before we get through with this life of Nephi we shall have occasion to dwell more at length upon their spirit and conduct. But upon this occasion Lehi became aroused. He was filled with the Spirit of the Lord to such an extent, and spoke unto them with such power, that their frames shook before him, and they were so confounded they dare not say anything against him; but they did as he commanded them.

CHAPTER III.

FAITH OF NEPHI AND ITS EFFECTS—SAM'S BELIEF—REVE-
LATION WITH PROMISE TO NEPHI—LAND OF PROMISE,
CHOICE ABOVE OTHER LANDS—NEPHI TO BE A RULER AND
A TEACHER TO HIS BRETHREN—REQUIRED TO RETURN TO
JERUSALEM—HIS WILLINGNESS—LEHI GRATIFIED AT HIS
FAITH—LABAN AND BRASS PLATES—ANGRY, AND REFUSED
TO GIVE THEM TO LAMAN—THREATENED HIS LIFE—LAMAN
AND LEMUEL DISCOURAGED—NEPHI'S PROPOSITION—HIS
BROTHERS AGREE TO IT.

IT is at this point we begin to get an insight into Nephi's
character. He was, as he tells us, exceeding young, though
large in stature, yet he had great desires to know of the mys-
teries of God, and he cried unto the Lord. The Lord visited
him and softened his heart, and he believed all the words of
his father. This kept him from rebeling against his father as
his two brothers had done. He told his brother Sam what the
Lord had manifested unto him by His Holy Spirit, and he
believed his words. From all that has come down to us concerning this older brother of Nephi's, Sam, he was a man of great
worth, not an aspiring, jealous, envious man, but humble,
believing, obedient, steadfast, true and faithful. He was not
gifted like his brother Nephi; but, though older, he recognized
Nephi's authority, submitted to his direction and counsel,
received his teachings and always stood by him in all the dis-
sensions and difficulties which the unbelief, jealousy and envy
of their two oldest brothers created.

Nephi also told Laman and Lemuel that which the Lord had
shown him ; but it was of no avail. They did not believe him.
Their unbelief grieved him, and he cried unto the Lord for
them. The Lord then blessed him because of his faith, and
said to him that he had sought Him diligently with lowliness
of heart. He told him further that, if they would keep His

commandments, they would prosper, and they should be led to the land of promise, a land which He had prepared for them, and which was choice above other lands; but if his brethren should rebel against him, they should be cut off from the presence of the Lord; if he, Nephi, would keep His commandments he should be made a ruler and a teacher over his brethren. He also told him at this time that in the day his brethren should rebel against Him, the Lord, He would curse them with a sore curse, and they should have no power over the children of Nephi, except they should also rebel against Him; and if they should rebel against Him, they should be a scourge unto them to stir them up in the ways of remembrance. From this we see that the Lord had chosen Nephi to be the ruler and teacher of his brethren, and this in consequence of his faith in seeking Him, and because of their iniquities.

In this revelation to Nephi appears for the first time in the record any allusion to the land of promise, the choice land above all others, which He destined them to inhabit. Doubtless the Lord had already revealed this to Lehi. But it does not appear. Nephi informs us there were many things his father had written that he had seen in visions and dreams and that he had prophesied about, which he, Nephi, had not given a full account of.

The selection by the Lord of Nephi to be their ruler and their teacher was always a cause of anger and trouble to Laman and Lemuel. They themselves never lived in a way to entitle them ei'her to rule or teach; and yet they were never heartily willing that Nephi should do so. Laman had the birthright as the oldest son, but he did not put himself in a position to exercise the rights which belonged to it. It was with him as with Cain, to whom the Lord said: "If thou doest well, shalt thou not be accepted? And if thou doest not well, sin lieth at the door. And unto thee shall be his (speaking of Abel) desire and thou shalt rule over him."

Laman would not do well. The Lord could not, consistently with His attributes and laws, sustain him in his wrong doing and make him the ruler; and because Nephi did obey the Lord, and thereby obtained the leadership, both Laman and Lemuel hated him.

After communing with the Lord Nephi returned to his father's tent. Then Lehi told him of a dream which he had had, in which the Lord had commanded him to send Nephi and his brothers back to Jerusalem to get the record of the Jews and the genealogy of their forefathers which were engraven upon plates of brass, and were in the possession of a man by the name of Laban, who was, as well as Lehi, a descendant of Joseph. Lehi told Nephi that his brothers murmured at this request, and said it was a hard thing which he had required of them; but, he added, "I have not required it of them; it is a commandment of the Lord." He told Nephi to go and he should be favored of the Lord, because he had not murmured. Nephi replied that he would go and do what the Lord had commanded.

"For," said he, "I know that the Lord giveth no commandments unto the children of men, save he shall prepare a way for them that they may accomplish the thing which he commandeth them."

There is a volume of meaning in this memorable remark of Nephi's, and it furnishes us the key to the actions of his entire life and the unfailing success which attended all his movements. Though he was but a youth, this expression shows that already he was full of faith. When God commanded him, all hesitation and doubt disappeared. He was ready to do his part, perfectly satisfied that the Lord would make up all that was necessary. The record informs us that when Lehi heard these words, he was exceedingly glad, for he knew that his son had been blessed of the Lord. This must have been a great comfort to him under the circumstances. However rebellious and hard the older ones might be, now he was not entirely alone; for here was one, at least, who could understand and sustain him.

The four sons, Laman, Lemuel, Sam and Nephi, took their tents and started for Jerusalem. After reaching there they held a consultation, and decided to cast lots to know which of them should have an interview with Laban. The lot fell upon Laman, the oldest. He now had the opportunity to show his ability. But he had weakened himself before he started by his murmuring and calling this a hard thing to do. One could therefore guess beforehand how his attempt would result. He saw Laban in his house and had a talk with him, during which he asked him for the records which were engraved upon the plates of brass, and which also contained his father's genealogy. Laban got angry and would not let him have the records; but thrust him out, and called him a robber, and threatened to kill him. Laman ran away from him, glad doubtless to escape without injury. His account to his brothers of his reception made them all feel sorrowful, and the older ones concluded it was no use to try any more to get the brass plates, and they would return to their father. This was not Nephi's feeling. He had been sent for those records; the Lord had given the command; and he was determined to get them before he returned. He told his brothers that, as the Lord lived and they lived, they would not go back to their father until they had accomplished that which the Lord had commanded them. It was at this juncture, when obstacles had to be overcome and the others were ready to succumb to them, that Nephi's superiority began to exhibit itself. He had been humble and sought unto the Lord; now the Lord was giving him strength and bringing into exercise those qualities which made him the leader among his brothers. Instead of returning, he proposed they should go and gather up the gold and silver and other riches which their father had left, when he moved out, and take these to Laban in exchange for the plates. He pointed out to his brothers how necessary it was they should have these records. They needed them to preserve for their children the language of the fathers, as well as the words of their holy prophets which had been delivered to them by the Spirit and power of God from the beginning of the world up to that time. His reasoning and arguments had weight with them and they agreed to his plan.

CHAPTER IV.

LEHI'S RICHES—LABAN COVETS THEM—SENT HIS SERVANTS TO
KILL LAMAN AND HIS BROTHERS—THEY FLEE FOR THEIR
LIVES—NEPHI WHIPPED BY LAMAN AND LEMUEL—VISITED
BY AN ANGEL—LAMAN AND LEMUEL STILL MURMUR—
NEPHI LEADS THEM TO THE CITY WALLS—LABAN LYING
DRUNK—HIS SWORD—MOST FAMOUS WEAPON IN THE
WORLD—THOSE WHO HAVE SEEN IT—NEPHI CONSTRAINED
TO KILL LABAN—PERSONATES HIM AND OBTAINS PLATES
—HIS BROTHERS FRIGHTENED—LABAN'S SERVANT, ZORAM
—PROMISES TO GO WITH NEPHI INTO THE WILDERNESS.

THE record does not inform us in what position Lehi had left
his riches. We may reasonably conclude that he had left
them in a place of security; for his sons found gold and silver and
other valuable things, and carried them to Laban's house, and
proposed to him to give him these in exchange for the records.
Laban would not consent to give up the plates; but the property the young men offered for them was so very valuable
that, as the record says, he lusted after it and was determined
to have it. He therefore thrust them out, and sent his
servants to kill them, so that he might obtain their property.
To save their lives they had to leave their valuables and make
the best of their way out of the city. They fled into the wilderness and thus escaped and hid in the cavity of a rock.
Laman by this time got angry. We are not told that he got
angry at Laban; but at his father and Nephi; and he made
Lemuel angry also. They said a good many hard things and
then they whipped Nephi with a rod, and we should infer that
Sam got a share of the beating. It is very probable that he
stood up for Nephi and defended him, and in that way incurred
their anger. While they were beating Nephi, an angel of the
Lord came and stood before them, and he said to them:

"Why do ye smite your younger brother with a rod? Know ye not that the Lord hath chosen him to be a ruler over you, and this because of your iniquities? Behold ye shall go up to Jerusalem again, and the Lord will deliver Laban into your hands."

After speaking to them the angel departed. We have heard of a good many people who have thought if they could only see an angel, and he should tell them anything, they would believe it, and never afterwards doubt it. Yet here were these two young men who had seen and been spoken to by an angel, and he had scarcely gone when they began to murmur. They did not believe that which the angel had told them; for they said:

"How is it possible that the Lord will deliver Laban into our hands? Behold, he is a mighty man, and he can command fifty, yea even he can slay fifty; then why not us?"

We can judge from this language how little they knew about God, or His power. Nephi again had to become their teacher. He encouraged them to go up again to Jerusalem, and to be faithful in keeping the commandments of the Lord; for, said he, He is mightier than all the earth, and of course mightier than Laban and his fifty, or even his tens of thousands. He quoted to them what Moses had done, and asked them how they could doubt when an angel had spoken to them. After all that he said they were still angry and still murmured, yet they followed him until they came to the outside of the walls of the city. Nephi got them to hide themselves outside the walls. Then he, by himself, crept into the city. He had no plan arranged beforehand as to what he would do. He trusted entirely to the Lord and was led by the Spirit. He went in the direction of Laban's house. As he drew near there he saw a man lying on the ground, who proved to be Laban, full of wine, and drunk. He had on a sword, which Nephi drew from the sheath and examined. He has given us a description of this weapon, the most famous of any that we have any account of. It served afterwards as his model when he found himself under the necessity of manufacturing swords with which to arm his people to defend themselves against the attacks of his brothers and their children: he also wielded it on more than one occasion in battle; and it was handed down among his descendants from generation to generation, being kept with their sacred records. It is still in existence, and besides being seen by the prophet Joseph, was shown to the three witnesses of the Book of Mormon—Oliver Cowdery, David Whitmer and Martin Harris—with the plates, the breastplate, the Urim and Thummim and the miraculous directors which were given to Lehi, and of which we shall say more as we proceed. The hilt of this sword was of pure gold and the workmanship was exceedingly fine; the blade was of the most precious steel.

After drawing the sword, Nephi was constrained by the Spirit to kill Laban. But he said in his heart: "Never at any time have I shed the blood of man," and he shrunk from the thought, and desired that he might not kill him. The Spirit said unto him again: "Behold the Lord hath delivered him into thy hands." Nephi knew that Laban had sought to take his and his brother's lives; that he was a murderer at heart; he knew that he would not hearken to the commandments of the Lord, and that he also had robbed them of their property. All these thoughts would pass through his mind at such a time. The Spirit said unto him again: "Slay him, for the Lord hath delivered him into thy hands. Behold, the Lord slayeth the wicked to bring forth his righteous purposes. It is better that one man should perish, than that a nation should dwindle and perish in unbelief." These words brought to his mind the words of the Lord to him in the wilderness, to the effect that inasmuch as his seed should keep His commandments, they should prosper in the land of promise. He also thought that they could not keep the commandments of the Lord according to the law of Moses, unless they should have the law. Nephi knew that that law was engraved upon the plates of brass. He also knew that the Lord had delivered Laban into his hands that he might obtain the records as He had commanded. His reluctance to shed blood was strong; but the voice of the Spirit was stronger, and he obeyed it. He took Laban by the hair of the head, and he cut off his head with his own sword. He then took his garments and put them upon himself and girded his armor about his loins. Then going forth to the treasury of Laban he saw Laban's servant who had the keys of the treasury. Him he commanded in the voice of Laban to go with him. The servant, seeing the dress and the sword, supposed it was Laban, and addressed him accordingly. He spoke to him about the elders of the Jews, for he knew that Laban had been out by night among them. Nephi replied to him as though he was Laban, and he also spoke to him about carrying the plates of brass to his brethren who were outside the walls, and ordered him to follow him. The servant thought he spoke of the brethren of the church, and still thinking it was Laban, followed him. While they were going to where Nephi's brothers were outside the walls, the servant kept up his conversation concerning the elders of the Jews, and it was not until they came in sight of Laman, Lemuel and Sam that he found out his mistake. When these latter saw two men coming towards them, and one of them Laban, as they supposed, they were frightened and ran. They imagined that Laban, having killed Nephi, had now come to kill them. It was only when Nephi called to them and made himself known to them, that they stopped. In the meantime, Laban's servant began to tremble, and he would have run back into the city, had not Nephi prevented him. Nephi was a large man and he had received much strength from the Lord, and when he saw the man's inclination to run away, he seized him and held him fast. Nephi gave him his oath that he need not be afraid, that if he would listen unto them, they would spare his life, and that if he would go down with them into the wilderness, he should be a free man such as they were. He told him that the Lord had commanded them to do what they had done; and should they not be diligent in keeping the commandments of the Lord? He said to him again, that if he would go with them into the wilderness to his father he should have a place among them. Zoram was this servant's name. Nephi's words gave him courage: he promised he would go with them, and he gave them his oath that he would remain with them from that time forward. Faithfully was that oath kept. At no time do we hear anything respecting Zoram faltering in his devotion to Nephi. He was ever his true friend, and his descendants were numbered with the descendants of Nephi.

CHAPTER V.

THE STATUS OF ZORAM—LAW OF MOSES RESPECTING BOND-MEN—CHARACTER OF LABAN—ADVANTAGES OF TAKING ZORAM INTO THE WILDERNESS.

THERE was one expression used by Nephi, which would lead us to suppose that Zoram was a bondman. He promised him freedom if he would go with them into the wilderness. This was evidently said to him as an inducement to comply with their wishes. There would be no special attraction in such a proposition to a man already free; but, to a bondman, the promise of being made as free as they were, would go a long way towards reconciling him to submit to their wishes. It may be asked, then, was Zoram one of the heathens or a son of one of the strangers who sojourned in the midst of Israel? for these only were the children of Israel permitted by the law of Moses to make perpetual bondmen.

We are aware that the law of Moses expressly commanded the children of Israel to keep no Hebrew servant whom they might buy, because of his poverty, for any longer period than six years; in the seventh year he should go out free for nothing, and be furnished liberally, by his master that had been, out of all the property the Lord had given him. There was only one condition, under the law of Moses, upon which one of the children of Israel could keep his brother in his service as a bondman; and that was by the free consent of the man himself. The law said that if in the seventh year, the man who had been bought, and who was at that time entitled to his release, should plainly say he would not go away from his master because he loved him and his family and was satisfied with him, then the master should take an awl and "thrust it through his ear unto the door," and he should then be his servant forever. The Lord was strict upon this point, for He viewed all the children of Israel as His servants, and they were not to be bought and sold as bondsmen. nor to be ruled over with rigor by their brethren. If, therefore, Zoram was an Israelite, as we fully believe he was, and the law of Moses had been strictly observed in Jerusalem at that time, the offer made by Nephi to make him a free man would have had no particular inducement to him; for, in any event, he would have been free at the end of six years. or if he had surrendered himself for life to Laban as his servant, and his ear had been bored with an awl, he had done so for love of Laban and his family and because he was pleased with the service. But, as we shall show, the law of Moses was not observed on this point in Jerusalem at that time. Laban was just such a man as would violate that law. He was a greedy, rapacious, cruel man, ready to take any advantage to gain his ends, even to shedding blood. Laman, Nephi's brother, must have known him well, and he said, "he can command fifty, yea even he can slay fifty." If he would not hesitate to murder these four young men, whom it is but reasonable to conclude he must have known were his kindred, being of the same lineage as himself, for their property, he would not scruple to enslave his poor brethren, or even to kill them on some pretext, if it suited his purpose to do so. The glimpse which Nephi gives of the condition of affairs in that city is sufficient to show us how little human life was valued. Men were stoned, and killed in other ways, were treated as though they had no rights which ought to be respected. because they warned the people to repent and prophesied if they did not, they would be visited by terrible judgments. There can be little doubt from Laban's character that he was one of these vindictive persecutors. It is very likely that he was a man who prided himself on his zeal for religion; for it is plain he went into the society of the elders of his people; yet he could get drunk, he could rob and try to murder. and still justify himself for such conduct as persecutors of the righteous do in these days. There can scarcely be any doubt about Lehi and he being acquainted. They were of the same lineage, residents of the same city, and Lehi knew that he had the records on the brass plates. Was not the repugnance of Laman and Lemuel to obey the command of the Lord through their father for them

to return to Jerusalem and get these records from Laban, and
their remark that it was "a hard thing" which their father
required of them, due, in part at least, to the fact that they
knew Laban and knew how he felt towards the family because
of their father's predictions? And is it not probable that one
reason for his treating Nephi and his brothers as he did, and
trying to kill them, was that he knew them as the sons of
Lehi, and was satisfied he could justify himself for anything
he might do to them, even if he murdered them? His conduct towards them was not that of a novice in crimes against
innocent people; but whether he had helped shed innocent
blood or not, the Lord knew that he had only failed in killing
Nephi and his brothers through the inability of his servants
to catch them, and He deemed him unfit to live and commanded Nephi to kill him. If he had been accessory to
murder, the law of the Lord through Moses was very plain as
to what his fate should be. The Lord says (*Numbers xxxv.*,
33), "For blood it defileth the land; and the land cannot be
cleansed of the blood that is shed therein, but by the blood
of him that shed it." Such a man as he would be a hard
master, and it is scarcely improper to suppose that Zoram was
the more content to accompany Nephi, because of the promise
held out to him of a release from servitude. The Prophet
Jeremiah, who knew all about the condition of affairs at Jerusalem during these days, speaks thus:

"Thus saith the Lord, the God of Israel : I made a covenant
with your fathers in the day that I brought them forth out of
the land of Egypt, out of the house of bondmen, saying,

"At the end of seven years let ye go every man his brother
an Hebrew, which hath been sold unto thee; and when he
hath served thee six years, thou shalt let him go free from
thee: but your fathers hearkened not unto me, neither inclined
their ear.

"And ye were now turned, and had done right in my sight,
in proclaiming liberty every man to his neighbor; and ye had
made a covenant before me in the house which is called by my
name :

"But ye turned and polluted my name, and caused every
man his servant, and every man his handmaid, whom he had

set at liberty at their pleasure, to return, and brought them into subjection, to be unto you for servants and for handmaids."

For breaking this covenant Jeremiah, inspired of the Lord, pronounced upon the nation, from the king down, terrible curses, and they were all fulfilled. From Jeremiah's words it is clear that Israelites were made bondmen by their brethren, and from Zoram's subsequent marriage and life we think it safe to assume that he was not an alien but an Israelite. Elder Orson Pratt thought that, from his being worthy to hold the keys of the treasury and of the sacred brass plates, Zoram was probably of the same tribe as Laban.

The determination of Nephi to take Zoram with them was clearly a matter of necessity. Nephi says they were desirous he should tarry with them that the Jews might not know concerning their flight into the wilderness, lest they should pursue and destroy them. When Zoram had made an oath to stay with them, their fears concerning him ceased. Two results were accomplished by having Zoram go with them. Their company was strengthened by the addition of one who proved himself a worthy man, and all clue to the cause of Laban's death and to the person who slew him was completely removed beyond reach of the Jews. The disappearance of Zoram, of Laban's clothing, armor, sword and records left the people of Jerusalem at liberty to frame whatever theory they chose respecting his death. There is no room to suppose that Nephi or his brothers were suspected of having had anything to do with it, for it does not appear that any of Laban's servants were present when they requested him to give them the records in exchange for their property, though they were afterwards told to chase and kill them. Had the names of Nephi and his brothers been associated with the death of Laban and the taking of the records, he was so prominent a man, and the circumstances of his death so widely known that they could not have visited Jerusalem again (which they did shortly afterwards) and induced another family to accompany them in the wilderness, with the least safety.

CHAPTER VI.

RETURN INTO WILDERNESS—JOY OF LEHI AND SARIAH
—LEHI A VISIONARY MAN—SARIAH'S GRIEF AND MUR-
MURING—HER SUBSEQUENT TESTIMONY—SACRIFICE AND
BURNT OFFERINGS—THE BRASS PLATES—THEIR CON-
TENTS—LEHI A DESCENDANT OF JOSEPH—VALUE OF
THESE RECORDS TO HIS DESCENDANTS—ANOTHER COLONY
OF JEWS—LOST KNOWLEDGE OF HEBREW LANGUAGE
AND OF GOD—NEPHI A GREAT BENEFACTOR—HE AND
BROTHERS AGAIN REQUIRED TO VISIT JERUSALEM—
ISHMAEL AND FAMILY—LAMAN AND LEMUEL STIR UP
MUTINY—WANT TO RETURN TO JERUSALEM—BIND NEPHI
—INTEND TO LEAVE HIM TO PERISH—NEPHI'S PRAYER—
HIS BANDS BURST—THE OTHERS PLEAD FOR HIM—
REVULSION OF FEELING ON PART OF HIS BROTHERS—
BEG HIS FORGIVENESS—REJOIN LEHI AND SARIAH—
THANKSGIVING AND SACRIFICES AND BURNT OFFER-
INGS.

THE return of the young men to the tent of Lehi in the
wilderness, was a cause of great joy to their parents,
and especially to their mother, Sariah. She had mourned with
all a mother's anxiety for them, supposing that they had
perished in the wilderness. Possessed of this idea, and thinking doubtless of the comforts they had left at Jerusalem, she
had, while they were gone, complained against Lehi and called
him a visionary man, accused him of bringing them from their
home, and now her sons were dead, and they themselves
would perish in the wilderness. This style of talk must have
been very unpleasant for Lehi. It was bad enough to endure
the taunts and persecutions of the Jews, and the unbelief and
stubborness of his eldest sons; but how very painful to witness
the tears and deep grief of his wife, and to hear her make
such accusations as these! He did what he could to comfort

her; for, like others who yield to such a spirit—she felt as badly over the imaginary loss of her sons and over her own and husband's death, as if she would never see her sons alive again, and as if she and Lehi were about to perish. He told her he knew he was a visionary man ; for if he had not seen the things of God in a vision, he would not have known the goodness of God, but had remained in Jerusalem and perished. Now he rejoiced in having obtained a land of promise. As for their sons, he knew that the Lord would deliver them from Laban, and bring them safely back to them in the wilderness.

The return of her sons comforted Sariah ; she saw that her reproaches and fears had been without cause, and she bore testimony that she knew the Lord had commanded her husband to come into the wilderness, and that He had also protected her sons and delivered them out of the hands of Laban, and given them power to accomplish that which He had commanded them. No doubt all were happy—Lehi and Sariah in having their children restored to them alive and well, and their sons at their escape and safe return with the brass plates for which they had been sent, and Zoram that he was a free man. Sacrifice and burnt offerings were offered unto the Lord by them and they gave thanks unto Him. An examination by Lehi of the records upon the plates disclosed their great value. They contained the five books of Moses, including an account of the creation of the world, and of Adam and Eve, our first parents; also a record of the Jews from the beginning to the commencement of King Zedekiah's reign ; also the prophecies of the holy prophets during the same period, and also many prophecies which had been spoken by Jeremiah. He also found upon them a genealogy of his fathers. He was, as this proved, a descendant of Joseph, who was sold by his brethren and carried as a bondman into Egypt. Laban also was of the same descent. He and his father had kept the records, and probably because they were an older branch of the family. While looking at these things the spirit of prophecy rested upon Lehi concerning his seed, and he predicted many things in relation to them ; among others, that these plates of brass should go forth unto all nations, kindreds, tongues and people who were of his seed; therefore they should never perish, nor be dimmed any more by time.

These records proved invaluable to that portion of Lehi's family who strove to keep the commandments of the Lord; for by their means they were kept from falling into many errors, and a knowledge of the things of God was kept before them. Another colony of Jews left Jerusalem eleven years after Lehi, and they were also led to this continent; but they had no records with them. Their language became so corrupted that when they were found by the descendants of Nephi, sometime near the close of the fourth or the beginning of the fifth century, after Lehi left Jerusalem, they could not understand their language. Not only had they lost the knowledge of the Hebrew language; but they had lost the knowledge of God and denied His being. We find several allusions throughout the Book of Mormon, by prominent men among the Nephites, to the great value of these plates and to the benefits the records they contained had been to the nation. Thus it is that the faith and energy of one man has frequently been of immense importance to future generations and peoples. To Laman and Lemuel the possession of these plates was not worth struggling or taking any risks for; so far as they were concerned posterity could go without them. But not so with Nephi. His willingness to do as the Lord commanded, and his determination not to be baffled, even though he incurred the risk of losing his life, opened his eyes to see the importance of these records. He was a great benefactor in this respect to his posterity, and the descendants also of his brothers reaped many advantages from them, and in days to come they will still prove a great blessing to them. It is frequently the case that, by apparently small and insignificant means, the Lord brings to pass great and important results. The obtaining of these plates was of incalculable benefit in maintaining and spreading the true civilization of the Nephite nation.

Shortly after the return of Nephi and his brothers to their parents, the Lord again spoke to Lehi, and gave him a commandment that they should proceed once more to Jerusalem and bring down Ishmael and his family into the wilderness. The reason for this was that it was not proper that

Lehi should take his family into the wilderness alone: but that his sons should have wives, so that they could have children in the land of promise. Their mission was successful. They spoke the words of the Lord unto Ishmael, and the Lord gave them favor in his sight and softened the hearts of himself and household, and they returned with them to Lehi's camp. We are not informed exactly what the number of Ishmael's family was; but we are led to suppose that it consisted of himself and wife, two sons who also had families, and five unmarried daughters. There may have been more than these; but if so they are not mentioned. It is believed by many, upon the authority of a remark which the Prophet Joseph is said to have made, that Ishmael was a descendant of Joseph. We did not hear the Prophet make this statement, but we feel assured it is so from the testimony of Elder Franklin D. Richards, who heard him say that such was the case. The blood of Ephraim was thus brought to this continent.

While they were traveling from Jerusalem to where Lehi was encamped, Laman and Lemuel had another outbreak. Who was the cause of it we are not told; but they and two of the daughters and two of the sons of Ishmael and the families of the latter, combined against Nephi, Sam, Ishmael and his wife, and their three daughters. They wanted to return to Jerusalem. Nephi, in speaking of this disturbance, calls their conduct, "rebellion." Whether Laman and Lemuel were restive and angry because of his superiority, as they often were subsequently, or not, we are not informed. But Nephi spoke to his brothers as though they were the leaders in this attempt to split the company and return to Jerusalem. He said that as his elder brothers they should not put him, the younger, under the necessity of speaking to them as he did and setting them an example. He appealed strongly to them, and warned them as to what their fate would be if they should return to Jerusalem. But his words only aroused their anger. It got to such a pitch that they seized and tied him fast with cords, with the design to leave him in the wilderness to be devoured by wild beasts.

There is no spirit so cruel and inhuman as that which prompts men to fight against the truth. Under its influence they go to the most extreme lengths. They will tell the most abominable lies, resort to every kind of violence, and shed the blood of innocence, even of those who are their nearest and best friends, and all this apparently, as though they were doing praiseworthy acts. It was this spirit which stirred up men in days of old to kill the prophets and to crucify the Son of God, and it is the same spirit which has prompted men in these days to persecute and kill the Prophets and Saints of God. What an awful act of cruelty this was which they proposed, to leave their youngest brother, a mere boy, tied hand and foot to be devoured by wild beasts! But their design was not to be accomplished. The Lord was near Nephi. He cried unto Him for deliverance and asked for strength to burst the bands with which he was fastened. He had no sooner offered his prayer than it was granted. The bands were loosed from his hands and feet, and he stood before them and spoke to them again. Their anger was not appeased even at this. They tried to get hold of him again. Then several of the company interposed. One of the girls and her mother and also one of the sons of Ishmael plead with them on his behalf. They succeeded in turning them from their purpose. A revulsion of feeling followed. They became sorrowful for what they had done, and bowed down before Nephi and begged him to forgive them; but he told them to pray to the Lord for forgiveness. They did so, and the journey was resumed. We may be sure that Lehi and Sariah felt very happy to see once more their sons with their old neighbors, Ishmael, and wife and their family and to have such an addition to their company. Thanks were offered unto the Lord, as well as sacrifice and burnt offering.

CHAPTER VII.

LEHI'S DREAM, OR VISION—REJOICES BECAUSE OF NEPHI
AND SAM—FEARS CONCERNING LAMAN AND LEMUEL—
HIS ENTREATIES TO THEM—GATHERED SEEDS AND GRAIN
—FIVE MARRIAGES—LEHI HAD FAITHFULLY KEPT COM-
MANDMENTS OF THE LORD—NEPHI'S DEVELOPMENT—
EXPERIENCE IN WILDERNESS NECESSARY TO PREPARE
COLONY FOR THE FUTURE—LEHI COMMANDED TO TRAVEL—
MIRACULOUS BRASS BALL, CALLED LIAHONA—HOW IT
OPERATED—TRAVEL IN S. S. E. DIRECTION—HUNT
FOR GAME—LED THROUGH MOST FERTILE PARTS OF THE
DESERT.

WHILE they were still encamped in the valley of Lemuel,
Lehi had a very important dream, or vision, which caused
him to rejoice because of Nephi and Sam ; for he had reason
to suppose that they and many of their posterity would be
saved. He told Laman and Lemuel that he feared exceedingly
because of them. He related what he had seen to his family,
and he exhorted Laman and Lemuel, with all the feeling of a
father who loved his children and was anxious for their salva-
tion, to hearken to his words. He preached and prophesied
unto them, and bade them keep the commandments of the
Lord, that they might not be cast off from His presence. He
also continued his conversation to his family upon other sub-
jects connected with the Jews and their future. Nephi also
about this time had remarkable manifestations given by the
Lord to him.

It is evident they remained in this valley of Lemuel for some
time. Whether they cultivated the ground and raised crops
we are not informed ; but we are informed by Nephi in his
record, directly after he and his brothers had returned
accompanied by Ishmael and his family, to his father's camp in
the valley of Lemuel, that they "had gathered together all
manner of seeds of various kinds, both of grain of every kind,

2

and also of the seeds of fruit of every kind." While they
were yet in this valley of Lemuel five marriages were arranged
and consummated. Nephi and his three brothers took each a
daughter of Ishmael to wife, and Zoram married the eldest
daughter. We may well suppose that Nephi married the girl
who plead so earnestly in his behalf on the journey from
Jerusalem, when his brothers were so enraged as to desire to
take his life. Such love and devotion as she then exhibited
would be likely to awaken feelings of admiration in him for
her, even if no more tender feeling had been in his breast
before.

Thus far Lehi had faithfully fulfilled all the commandments
of the Lord which he had received. He had forsaken his
home, had launched into the wilderness with his family, had
obtained the necessary records to preserve the knowledge of
God and all the prophecies of the holy prophets, had his
company strengthened by the addition of Ishmael and his
family, and now had the gratification of seeing his sons united
to wives. The Lord had been with him and blessed him, and
he was now in a better condition to cut loose from the rest of
the world and to fulfill the destiny the Lord had in store for
him and his people than when he first escaped from Jerusalem.
His stay in the valley of Lemuel had, therefore, been necessary to
effect these preparations. Nephi also during this period had
emerged from boyhood to manhood. Under the influence of
the Spirit and revelations of the Lord, his character had rapidly
developed. Though young in years he was now an experienced
man, full of that confidence, self-reliance and fearlessness which
the consciousness of being a servant of the Lord, of being
acknowledged and sustained as such by Him, always brings.
However weak he might be himself, he knew that in the
strength of the Lord he could accomplish whatever might be
required of him. His energy, robust faith and willing
obedience must have been a great comfort and help to his
father in those days. Nephi had this advantage: he was young
and vigorous, and could the more readily adapt himself to the
new methods of life which they had to adopt in the wilderness;
while Lehi, more advanced in years, would find traveling in
this wild and desert country, and enduring the hardships they

had to encounter, a very great change from the mode of life to which he had been accustomed in Jerusalem. Though they were now in these favorable circumstances for the prosecution of the enterprise required of them by the Lord, they had yet to gain an experience, hard and trying to their feelings and faith, without which they would not be fully prepared for that which they had to do. Their forefathers, after escaping from Egypt under the leadership of Moses, were not permitted to enter into and possess the land at once. They had to wander in the wilderness for forty years. It was not necessary that so much time should be consumed by the children of Israel in going from Egypt to Canaan; but it was necessary that, before entering into that land and changing from a condition of slavery, such as they occupied in Egypt, under the iron rule of Pharaoh, to that of a free people—rulers in fact—with full power to enact and execute laws to govern themselves, their land and the surrounding peoples, they should have experience. Stubborn and rebellious as they were, it required forty years to give them the necessary schooling, during which period all who, at the time they left Egypt, were over twenty years of age—with two notable exceptions, Caleb and Joshua—passed off and a new generation took their places. So in the case of Lehi and family and company, they needed training, though not for so long a period as their forefathers. While they were inexperienced, trifles annoyed and worried them; they had not learned to patiently endure and submit to privations and hardships. Their previous lives had been passed, doubtless, in circumstances of ease and plenty: want had been unknown to them; but they now had to lead a new life; the comforts to which they had been accustomed they had to dispense with and not complain at their loss. In the beginning of their experience in the wilderness many things were viewed as afflictions and dreadful to bear which, after a few years of such life, they scarcely noticed; so easy is it for people, especially if sustained by the Spirit of the Lord and the knowledge that they are obeying His requirements, to accommodate themselves to new circumstances and conditions of life.

After all these preparations had been made in the valley of Lemuel, the voice of the Lord came to Lehi, in the night, and commanded 'him to take his journey into the wilderness the next day. When he arose in the morning and went to the door of his tent, to his great astonishment he saw, lying upon the ground, a fine brass ball of curious workmanship. Within the ball were two spindles; one of these pointed the way they should go in the wilderness. This ball, or director, was called Liahona, the interpretation of which is, a compass. But it differed in several respects from what are known as compasses.*

We are told by Alma the prophet that "there cannot any man work after the manner of so curious a workmanship." It was prepared by the Lord to show unto Lehi and his company the course which they should travel in the wilderness. And it worked for them according to their faith in the Lord—the pointers moving according to the faith, and diligence and heed which they gave unto them. There was another peculiarity about this curious instrument: there was written upon these pointers a writing plain to be read, which gave them understanding concerning the ways of the Lord; and this was written and changed from time to time, according to the faith and diligence which they gave unto it. Had they always paid strict attention to this writing, and not been slothful and careless, they would have traveled a direct course, and made greater progress in the wilderness, and would not have been so much

---

*——In this connection it may be of interest to say a few words about what is known as the mariner's compass. It is claimed that the Chinese used the compass at a very early period; and it is thought probably that Marco Polo, the traveler, introduced it to Europe from China, about 1290 A. D., twelve years before Gioja, of Amalfi, its supposed inventor.

"Some people contend that the compass is no new invention; but that the ancients were acquainted with it. They say that it was impossible for Solomon to have sent ships to Ophir, Tarshish and Parvaim, without this useful instrument. They insist that it was impossible for the ancients to be acquainted with the attractive virtue of the magnet, and to be ignorant of its polarity; nay, they affirm that this property of the magnet is plainly mentioned in the book of Job, where the loadstone is mentioned by the name of *topaz, or the stone that turns itself.*" Ency. Brit.

afflicted by hunger and thirst; but Laman and Lemuel and their brothers-in-law, the sons of Ishmael, were frequently in transgression. The children of Israel were led through the wilderness in the days of Moses "by the pillar of cloud by day and the pillar of fire by night." We are told that "God went before them by day in a pillar of cloud to lead them the way." In like manner the Lord designed that Lehi and his company should be lead by the compass which had been so wonderfully given them.

After receiving the compass they gathered up all that they could carry with them, and the remainder of the provisions which the Lord had given them, and seed of every kind, and their tents, and crossing the river Laman, they traveled for four days, in nearly a south by south-east direction until they came to a place which they called Shazer. Here they camped until they could hunt for game to sustain their families. We suppose that in the wilderness in this neighborhood wild animals were numerous, and they, therefore selected it as a temporary stopping place. Their method of hunting was with bows and arrows, stones and slings. After collecting what they had killed they returned to their families at Shazer. From this place they traveled in the same course—S.S.E.—following the direction of the compass, which led in the most fertile parts of the desert, and which were near the Red Sea.

CHAPTER VIII.

TRAVEL IN DESERT—KILL GAME BY THE WAY—
UNCOOKED MEAT THEIR FOOD—NEPHI BREAKS HIS
BOW—FAILS TO OBTAIN FOOD—LAMAN AND OTHERS
COMPLAIN BITTERLY—LEHI, ALSO, MURMURS—NEPHI
KEEPS HIS PATIENCE AND COURAGE—REMONSTRATES
WITH HIS BROTHERS—MAKES A WOODEN BOW—LEHI
VERY SORROWFUL—SEES WRITING ON THE BRASS BALL
—NEPHI GOES FOR GAME IN DIRECTION INDICATED—
COMPANY FILLED WITH JOY THROUGH HIS OBTAINING
FOOD—RESUME TRAVEL—ISHMAEL'S DEATH—HIS CHAR-
ACTER—OUTBREAK AND REBELLION OF PART OF HIS
CHILDREN AGAINST LEHI AND NEPHI—LAMAN PROPOSES
TO KILL THE TWO LATTER—ATTACHMENT TO BIRTHPLACE.

IN looking through the description of a journey in this
country by a traveler of the name of Wallin (Jour. of Geog.
Soc., 1854, page 161) we were struck with the remarkable
coincidence between the direction in which he traveled and
that traveled by Lehi and company, upwards of twenty-four
centuries before. He says:

"The direction was in general during the whole of our route
S.S.E., according to the rule which the people of that land
give a traveler about to traverse this desert, 'so to direct his
course that he always has the polar star on his left shoulder-
blade.'"

As they traveled they killed game by the way; occasionally
camping to rest and obtain more food. We are not told what
the wild animals were which they used for food; but in modern
times the gazelle, antelope and mountain goat are numerous in
that region, and are hunted by the Arabs; the flesh of the goat,
especially, is excellent. The ostrich also is common, partridges
and quails and pigeons of various kinds are plentiful, as also
wild ducks, along the coast of the Red Sea. Some of the
mountains in these days are said to abound in game. The ass

runs wild in many parts and is hunted by the Arabs, but only for the sake of his skin. Doubtless Lehi and his company found the game very abundant in places. These places would be selected for their camps while they rested and obtained new supplies; for meat was their principal if not sole diet while in the wilderness, and this uncooked, or raw. The Lord did not suffer them to make much fire, for He had said to them: "I will make thy food become sweet, that ye cook it not." It is probable that when they secured a quantity of game they dried the meat so that it would be lighter to carry and keep better; this they could do in that climate without the aid of fires.

At one of their camping places, where they had stopped for the purposes of resting and obtaining food, Nephi, while out hunting, had the misfortune to break his bow, which was made of fine steel. It seems from the effect this accident had upon his brothers, that Nephi was the best and most skillful hunter of the party and their chief dependence to procure them food. They were angry with him because he had broken his bow; "for," as the record says, "we did obtain no food." They had to return to their families without any, and as they were all much fatigued with traveling, they suffered considerably for the want of something to eat. This, added to their other privations and afflictions, was more than Laman and Lemuel and the sons of Ishmael would patiently bear. They complained bitterly of their sufferings; but bad feelings were not confined to them upon this sorrowful and trying occasion, even Lehi himself, "began to murmur against the Lord, his God." Though Nephi was afflicted with the rest, he did not lose his patience or self-control. He remonstrated with his brothers for their complaints against the Lord; and as their bows had lost their spring and appeared to be of no value as weapons of the chase, he found himself under the necessity of making a wooden bow and arrow. Having done this, and being provided with a sling and with stones, he asked his father in what direction he should go to obtain food. It seems that his energetic words and remonstrances had had the effect to cause them to humble themselves. It will be noticed that it was to his brothers his remonstrances were addressed. He had been

told that he should be their ruler and their teacher. It was
quite proper, therefore, that he should correct them. But not
so with his father. He was still his leader, and he looked up
to and honored him. Yet Lehi must have heard what he said
to his brethren, and his remarks must have had their effect
upon him.

Lehi saw his sin in murmuring against the Lord, and he was
chastened and brought down into the depths of sorrow. The
voice of the Lord said to him, in reply to his inquiry: "Look
upon the ball and behold the things which are written." We
are not told what was there written; but the effect of reading
it was to cause Lehi and his sons and Ishmael's sons and the
women to fear and tremble exceedingly. Nephi was directed
by the ball to go to the top of the mountain, where he succeeded
in killing several wild animals, which he carried back to camp.
Supplied once more with food, the people were filled with joy,
and they humbled themselves before the Lord, and gave Him
thanks.

For some time after leaving this camping place they traveled
S.S.E., and stopped at a suitable spot. Here Ishmael died, and
was buried at a place which was called Nahom. From all that is
said of Ishmael we should infer that he was a patient, humble
and faithful man. In all the outbreaks of his sons and two
daughters and sons-in-law, Laman and Lemuel, he is not
mentioned as giving them any support or countenance. On the
contrary, at the time the family was on the way from Jerusalem
to the valley of Lemuel, and Laman and Lemuel and his sons
and two daughters expressed the determination to go back to
Jerusalem. it was against Ishmael and wife, and three daughters
and Sam and himself, as Nephi informs us, they rebelled. It
is clear that he did not desire to go back. He had set his face
to serve the Lord and was determined, apparently, to obey
Him.

His death was a severe blow to his family. It was seized by
some of them as an occasion for another outbreak. His
daughters mourned exceedingly at his departure. This appeared
to them to be the climax of all their troubles. They had been
wandering for a long time in the wilderness; they had suffered
from hunger, thirst and fatigue; they had been afflicted with

the heat and doubtless with the poisonous siroccos of the desert: and now, to crown all, their father had died. and staring them in the face, there was the probability that they themselves would perish in the wilderness from hunger. Their murmuring and discontent found vent against Lehi. He was the author, they thought, of all their misery. He had led them away from their pleasant home at Jerusalem. He had launched them upon this new and distasteful life, and in this he had been aided by Nephi, whom they looked upon as being as bad as he. They wanted to return to Jerusalem. Two of these daughters of Ishmael were the wives of Laman and Lemuel. Nephi. Sam and Zoram had each a wife of the same family. It is not probable that these last indulged in these unreasonable and wicked feelings and talk. But without doubt the two former did, as well as their brother's wives. Laman was aroused by their grief and their complaints. They gave voice to the thoughts which he himself entertained. He therefore proposed to Lemuel and to his brothers-in-law, the sons of Ishmael, that they should kill his father, Lehi, and his brother, Nephi. He accused Nephi of taking it upon him to be their ruler and their teacher. They were his older brothers, and what right had he to do this? "Now." said he, "Nephi says the Lord has talked with him. and also that angels have ministered unto him. But, behold, we know he lies unto us. He tells us these things, and he worketh many things by his cunning arts. that he may deceive our eyes, thinking, perhaps, that he may lead us away unto some strange wilderness; and after he has lead us away, he has thought to make himself a king and a ruler over us, that he may do with us according to his will and pleasure." He and his father, he said, were alike. It was upon their ideas the company was acting and by which it was led.

This was Laman's method of arousing hatred against his father and brother. His plan was to kill them; then what would hinder him and those who thought as he did from getting control and leading the company back to Jerusalem? Their old home appeared to be ever in the thoughts of Laman and Lemuel. They seemed to entertain no doubts about its safety and prosperity, notwithstanding all that their father and

their brother Nephi had said to them upon the subject. It was
with great reluctance that they left their native city, Jerusalem.
They were never satisfied with their father for leading them
away from there. While indulging in their frequent fits of
murmuring they accused him of being visionary and of being
misled by his foolish imaginations.

CHAPTER IX.

POPULAR AT JERUSALEM TO REJECT PROPHETS—LAMAN AND LEMUEL DID NOT BELIEVE PREDICTIONS CONCERNING THAT CITY—CONFIDENCE OF JEWS IN JERUSALEM—GLORY OF THE CITY—THE MAGNIFICENT TEMPLE—CAPTURE OF THE CITY—THE CONSPIRATORS CHASTENED—LEHI AND NEPHI SAVED.

LAMAN and Lemuel were evidently full of the ideas which
were popular in Jerusalem at the time they lived there.
It was the popular thing at that time to reject the predictions
and warnings of Jeremiah and the other prophets concerning
the destruction of Jerusalem, the killing of many of its
inhabitants, and the carrying away captive of many unto
Babylon. We are warranted in believing that these young
men had but little faith in these predictions. They had a good
inheritance at Jerusalem. Their father, Lehi, was a man of
wealth there, having an abundance of gold and silver and other
precious things. They could see no sense in the movement
which he had made, in leaving his comfortable and pleasant
surroundings and taking his journey into the wilderness. At
no time during their wanderings do they appear to have had
any faith in what their father said should be the fate of
Jerusalem.

The confidence of the Jews in the city of Jerusalem and its
high destiny was something very extraordinary. Their great
men and prophets had rejoiced in the walls and bulwarks of its
glorious temple. They had uttered many promises and predictions concerning the city and its great destiny. These

utterances the Jews believed. The prophets who had spoken
and written them had passed away, but their memories were
cherished as sacred. New prophets arose, who prophesied evil
concerning the city, the temple and the people. They foretold
the disasters which should bafall them and the dreadful fate
that awaited them, unless the nation and its rulers should
speedily repent, These prophets the Jews rejected. They did
not believe Jeremiah; they did not believe Ezekiel; they did
not believe Lehi, nor any of the many prophets, who, Nephi
informs us, were raised up and sent by the Lord to them at
that time. But Josephus says, they did give credit to false
prophets, who deluded them with the statement that the king
of Babylon would make no more war against them; but that
the Egyptians, who were the allies of the Jews, would make
war against him and conquer him. The king of Babylon had
killed their king, Jehoiakim; he had taken away many cap-
tives; his son Jehoiachim, whom he had made king had also
been sent captive to Babylon, together with many thousands of
the leading people; the temple had been despoiled; and
Zedekiah himself, an uncle of the last king, and a brother of
King Jehoiakim, had been placed upon the throne by the
king of Babylon and only held the kingly dignity by his per-
mission; but yet, so confident were they of their future
prosperity, and, as Josephus informs us, so deluded by false
prophets as to the assistance Egypt would render them, that
they were heedless of all the predictions and warnings of the
true prophets of God and sought to take their lives. According
to Josephus:

"False prophets deceived Zedekiah in saying that the king
of Babylon would not make any more war against him or his
people; nor remove them out of their own country into
Babylon; and that those then in captivity would return, with
all those vessels of which the king of Babylon had despoiled
the temple."

It is very evident that Laman and Lemuel shared in these mis-
taken views. They had but little or no faith in their father's
words. The false prophets made statements and uttered
pretended prophecies which were more agreeable to their ears
and more in consonance with their ideas and anticipations.

Jerusalem had been chosen of God. It was His city. Tradition had pointed out one of the hills upon which it stood as the spot to which Abraham brought his son Isaac, upon that memorable occasion when, in obedience to divine command, he prepared to sacrifice him to the Lord. From the days of David it had been the political and religious capital of the Israelitish nation; that king had removed the ark of the covenant there. He had prepared gold and silver, brass and iron, dressed stones and cedar timber in abundance before his death for his son Solomon, with which to build the temple. Here was that glorious building which was adorned and beautified by the great King Solomon as no building had ever been—the house of God, which He had designed to fill with His glory. This structure, for its extent, elaborateness and grandeur, was not only the pride of all Israel, but the wonder of all people who saw it. In the temple was the great altar of sacrifice, the holy of holies, toward which the eyes of all the nation were turned as the point where the Lord revealed Himself to His servants. When Lehi and his family left Jerusalem the temple had been despoiled of much of its riches; but those celebrated works of molten brass, executed by Hiram, the Tyrian, with which Solomon had adorned it, the sea of ten cubits in diameter supported by twelve oxen, the bases, and the pillars Jachin and Boaz, each of them eighteen cubits in hight and twelve in circumference. which stood in the porch still remained there. It was not until the capture of the city by Nebuchadnezzar, king of Babylon, about eleven years after the departure of Lehi, that these were broken up, and the materials, with other rich plunder from the temple and from the city, carried to Babylon. Though in the days of Lehi, Jerusalem was not so magnificent as in the days of Solomon, yet it was still the splendid city of the great king. It had passed through many vicissitudes since that day. Ten of the tribes had seceded under Jeroboam and set up a rival capital at Samaria, yet to the Jew it was the holiest spot on earth; around it clustered the most glorious memories and the most brilliant hopes. The withdrawal of the allegiance and the tribute of the larger portion of the Israelitish race had not caused the kingly city to lose much of its splendor or of its influence among the nations.

The sons of Lehi were familiar with the history of their
birthplace. They knew that if it had declined through the
misrule of one monarch, it had been resuscitated through the
zeal of another. It was more than likely that Laman and
Lemuel had unshaken confidence in the skill and valor of their
nation in war; they knew how impregnably strong were the
fortifications, the towers and the walls of the sacred city; they
were aware that it was only by the consent of the two last
kings that the armies of the king of Babylon had effected their
entrance within its walls; but they were probably satisfied in
their own minds that, should the people of Jerusalem defend
their city, no army or means of attack which the king of
Babylon could bring against it would be successful in effecting
its capture, much less its destruction. They would not believe
that the city which the Lord had chosen, and which had a
histôric existence of five centuries before the hanging gardens
for which Babylon was famous were built, was to be destroyed
by the king of that city. But the Lord had pronounced its
doom. He had witnessed its wickedness and abominations.
His prophets had warned its people what their fate would be,
and there was only one way of escape—the contrite repentance
of its king, nobles and people, and thorough submission to the
will of the Lord. Eleven years after Lehi and his family left
Jerusalem the city was captured by Nebuchadnezzar; but so
formidable was its resistance that it could only be reduced by
starving its inhabitants. Lehi was shown its destruction in a
vision, and in telling his sons and all their families about it, he
said that had they remained in Jerusalem he and they would
also have perished.

The Lord did not suffer Lehi and Nephi to be injured by
these wicked children and brothers. He was with them, and
the voice of the Lord spoke many things unto the conspirators
and chastened them exceedingly. This caused their anger to
subside, and they repented of their sins, and once more they
were blessed with food and were saved from perishing.

CHAPTER X.

TRAVEL IN EASTERLY DIRECTION—LAND BOUNTIFUL—"IRRE-
ANTUM," OR MANY WATERS—EIGHT YEARS IN WILDER-
NESS—CHILDREN BORN—DIET OF RAW MEAT—WOMEN
HEALTY AND STRONG AS MEN—LEARN TO BEAR
JOURNEYINGS WITHOUT MURMURING—"ARABY THE
BLEST"—TRAVELERS' DESCRIPTION OF LAND—COMPANY
REST FOR MANY DAYS.

CONTENTED once more to be led, the company resumed
their journey in an easterly direction, until they came to a
land which they called Bountiful, because of the abundance of
its fruit and wild honey. This was on the sea shore. They
camped upon the shore and called the sea "Irreantum," the
meaning of which is many waters. The travels in the wilderness covered a space of eight years. During this period they
had children born to them, and although they lived upon raw
meat, their wives had plenty of milk with which to nurse
their children, and they were healthy and strong as the men,
and what is worthy of note, "they began to bear their journeyings without murmurings." This was a great point gained.
We do not have a full account of their trials and difficulties
while traveling for these eight years in that desert land; but
Nephi says they traveled and waded through much affliction;
indeed they suffered so many afflictions and so much difficulty,
they could not write them all. No doubt their new life called forth
their ingenuity and greatly tried their patience. It had made
them hardy and enduring, capable of bearing fatigue and of
contending with difficulty and hardship. The details of their
perplexities, and the shifts to which they were put, the Latter-
day Saints who made the journey from Nauvoo in the state of
Illinois to the Great Salt Lake Valley during the early years of the
settlement, can readily supply. Nephi takes the opportunity,
while speaking of their journey and the wonderful manner in
which they had been sustained, especially the women in the bearing
and nursing of their children, to call attention to the fact that

the commandments of God must be fulfilled; and if they are kept by the children of men, He doth nourish and strengthen them, and provides means whereby they can accomplish the thing which He has commanded them. This great truth Nephi never lost sight of, and it furnishes us, as we have said before, the key to his success in accomplishing the extraordinary works assigned to him.

The direction in which they traveled after the death of Ishmael is that which would lead a company to-day into the most fertile region in Arabia. One traveler in speaking of a region, if not that called by Lehi and his company Bountiful, certainly adjoining it, says:

"As we crossed these [open fields] with lofty almond, citron and orange trees, yielding a delicious fragrance on either hand, exclamations of astonishment and admiration burst from us. Is this Arabia? we said: this the country we had looked on heretofore as a desert? Verdant fields of grain and sugar cane, stretching along for miles, are before us; streams of water flowing in all directions, intersect our path; and the happy and contended appearance of the peasants, agreeable helps to fill up the smiling picture. The atmosphere was delightfully clear and pure; and as we trotted joyously along, giving or returning the salutation of peace or welcome, I could almost fancy I had reached that 'Araby the blest,' which I had been accustomed to regard as existing only in the fictions of our poets." Trav. in Arabia, Vol. I. pp. 115, 116.

Captain Haines, whose manuscript journal is quoted from in Forster's Arabia, p. 452, says of this part of Arabia:

"The whole province of Hydramant is represented as abundant in fertilization and richly covered hills; the palm groves, magnificent; plentiful supplies of water, and, indeed, every beauty and perfection necessary to make a paradise of this earth."

Palgrave, (Jour. of Geo. Soc. Vol. 34, 1864, p. 147) in speaking of the province of Batinah, in the district of Oman, says:

"Those lands lying between the sea and Jebel-Akhdar, are especially rich in produce, except were the rocky coast-line interferes."

He describes the trees of that region as the cocoanut, the date palms, the manga tree, and other fruit-bearing trees, and says, "it is indeed the garden of the Peninsula." Speaking of a district adjoining this, he describes fertile valleys, full of rich vegetation and considerable produce; vines, whose wine is said to be good, abound in the slopes. "Bees abound in the mountain, and furnish excellent honey of a whitish color" (p. 148).

The lapse of twenty-four centuries makes wonderful changes in the earth's surface, but here is a land which is to-day exactly answering the description which Nephi gave of it—a land to which, because of its much fruit and also wild honey, they gave the appropriate name of Bountiful. Not even the honey in the mountains is wanting to distinguish it to-day. This traveler, in speaking of the mountains of that region, says: "The mountains themselves are sometimes bare—more often wooded—at least partially so." No doubt the mountains were wooded at the time Lehi and company reached there; for Nephi, as we shall see as we proceed with our history, needed timber convenient to the sea. In general outline the Arabian sea-shore offers little variety, being mostly mountainous; but there are exceptions to this as we have seen. Some parts of this shore present regions of remarkable fertility. It doubtless did the same at the time of which we write. It was to one of these rich spots that Lehi and his company were led, and charming and attractive it must have appeared to them after their long and weary march, suffering from hunger and thirst, in the desert. With what peculiar feelings they must have gazed on the great ocean whose waves beat upon the shore where they were encamped! It is not difficult to understand that they "were exceedingly rejoiced" when they reached such a place, and that having reached there some of them felt as though they did not wish to go any further.

Some of the Latter-day Saints who left Nauvoo, and traveled, having but little rest, until they reached the valley where Salt Lake City now stands, felt as though they had had traveling enough to last for years. They were so fatigued with their journey and the hardships incident thereto that they felt delighted to reach a place where there was a prospect of having a relief from that kind of life. But how much more would this be the case with this company after their long and toilsome journey! They had reached an earthly paradise. No occasion now to hunt for game to supply food necessary for their wants. No suffering from hunger or thirst now. Here, upon all hands, was everything in profusion necessary to sustain life—fruit of the most delicious kind. Dates form the staple of Arab food to-day, and probably they had the Kholas date—for date palms abound in all that region—the fruit of which is amber-colored, and of exquisite flavor. This fruit called the king of dates, grows in a district near the sea, and is noted all over Arabia for its superiority over every other variety. An abundance of honey. Drinking water, sweet and plentiful. And fish, too; for that ocean is full of fish of almost every kind. If their past habits of eating meat should have caused them to tire of the fruit, game likely abounded in a fertile region like that and was easily procured. Here Nephi rested with the others "for the space of many days" before he was called upon to perform new labors—labors that were essential to the establishment of the purpose the Lord had in view for them.

CHAPTER XI.

HOW DID THEY TRAVEL?—HAD THEY VEHICLES?—CHILDREN
OF ISRAEL USED COVERED WAGONS—DID LEHI AND
COMPANY USE CAMELS?—EXPERIENCE OF BATTALION IN
CALIFORNIA—CUSTOM IN ABYSSINIA—LAMAN AND COM-
PANIONS NEVER FORGOT HABITS ACQUIRED IN THE
DESERT—TRANSMITTED THEM TO POSTERITY IN THEIR
NEW HOME—NEPHI CHERISHED TRUE KNOWLEDGE OF
CIVILIZATION—CONTRAST BETWEEN THE TWO BROTHERS
—EACH LEFT HIS IMPRESS UPON HIS NATION.

THERE is nothing said in the record which has come to us
respecting the method of traveling adopted by Lehi and
his company in the wilderness—whether they had beasts of
burden or conveyances of any kind, or not. That they did not
go afoot and carry upon their own backs that which they had
with them, is so plain, we think, that no one who reflects upon
the subject will entertain such an idea. In the first place we
learn that Lehi took no gold, silver, or other valuables with
him when he left Jerusalem, but he did take provisions and
tents. When his sons returned to Jerusalem to obtain the
plates they took with them their tents. In that climate a tent
at least was necessary for a covering. They certainly had some
means of carrying these provisions and tents. While they
were in the valley of Lemuel they gathered together seeds of
grain and fruit of every kind. When they left there they took
these with them, and they carried them with them during all
their wanderings; they also took with them "all the remainder
of our [their] provisions which the Lord had given unto"
them, and their tents. Besides these, they took "whatsoever
things we [they] should carry into the wilderness." These
would comprise their clothing, their weapons of the chase, and
other necessary articles. We think it is safe also to suppose
that, while they killed game by the way as they traveled, they
also accumulated a stock for future use when they stopped, as
they often did, to rest and to hunt. We scarcely think

they used vehicles for the purpose of transporting all these
articles. The character of the country would be unsuitable for
their use; though their forefathers, when they traveled in the
wilderness between the Red Sea and Canaan had wagons with
them and they used oxen to draw them.

We think that the popular impression is that the children of
Israel upon their journey to the promised land of Canaan knew
nothing about wagons and had no use for them. But the fact
is, they traveled in heavy marching order. They had their
wives, children, effects, and indeed all their worldly possessions
with them. Upon one occasion the princes of Israel, each a
representative of one of the tribes, brought an offering of six
covered wagons and twelve oxen and gave them to Moses.
That is they each gave an ox and half a wagon. These were
given to the Levites for their use (*Numbers vii.*, 2-9). In the
country which Lehi and his company were traveling it was
then the fashion, as it has been through all the intervening
centuries and still is, to use animals for carrying burdens. The
camel, "the ship of the desert," as he has been aptly called,
has proved of inestimable value for this purpose to the
inhabitants of the Arabian peninsula. Horses and asses attain
their greatest excellence in that land; they are, however, more
employed for riding than for loads. But the camel would be
of as great use to Lehi and his fellow-travelers as it was and
is to the Arabs. He and his sons must have known of its value
and its adaptability for the purposes they needed. We think
it very likely, therefore, that they used camels to carry their
baggage, and probably their wives and children and themselves. Travelers inform us that in pasture land Arabia is
singularly fortunate, and that the very desert supplies through
the greater part of its extent sufficient browse for camels.

Our views upon this point are sustained, we think, by the
experience of the Latter-day Saints in the mountains. When
they left Winter Quarters, their experience in traveling was
confined to the methods to which they had been accustomed;
but when those who had been in the Battalion and discharged
in California came to Salt Lake Valley, they brought with
them their baggage and provisions packed on horses and mules
—a method of traveling well suited to the country over which

they journeyed, and which they, with ready facility, had
adopted from the people of the land, the Californians. This
style of traveling has ever since been common in our land. Its
adoption by the members of the Battalion was, under the
circumstances, a most sensible thing; and had the same men
been placed in Arabia, and had seen or known anything about
the camel and his wonderful fitness for all the purposes of
traveling in that land, they would have used it with the same
readiness as they did the pack animals of California.

Referring again to the journey of the children of Israel in
the wilderness, the difficulty of providing water for their
numerous cattle has proved a great stumbling-block to many
people, especially to those inclined to doubt the truth of the
sacred record. A suggestion has been made upon this point
(Palmer's Desert of the Exodus, p. 272) that reduces this
stumbling-block considerably. Instead of cattle being an
encumbrance to the movements of the host, they could have
been used as beasts of burden. In addition to the camp furniture,
each could carry its own supply of water, sufficient for several
days, in water-skins slung at its sides, precisely as Sir Samuel
Baker, an English traveler, found them doing at the present
day in Abyssinia. Those who have traveled on our own deserts
know how common an occurrence it has been to carry water,
not in water-skins, but in kegs slung upon the sides of pack
animals. Though cattle could have been used in this manner
by Lehi and party, the country through which they traveled
was not so favorable for pasturage for them. But the camel
was at home there. He could live upon scanty herbage; he
could travel for days without water. From his hair they could
make tents and clothing, and in every respect he was a better
animal for their use than the ox.

In the matter of clothing, they doubtless learned to be very
simple. The climate was one which required but little.
Travelers describe the dress of the wandering Arabs of the
present day as consisting, on the part of the men, of a long
cotton shirt, open at the breast, and often girt with a leathern
girdle. A cloak of hair is sometimes thrown over the shoulders.
A handkerchief, folded but once, covers the head, round which
it is kept in its place by a piece of twine or twisted hairband.

To this costume a pair of open sandals is added. Among the Bedouins of the south a light wrapper takes the place of the handkerchief on the head, and a loin-cloth that of the shirt. The attire of the women is hardly more complicated. It is worthy of remark in this connection that the wicked portion of Lehi's descendants never forgot or threw off the habits of life which they had adopted in the wilderness. When they reached the promised land, the continent of South America, if they pursued agriculture at all it was only for a short time. At Lehi's death, if not before, they resumed their old nomadic habits. They had been a wandering tribe of people for eight years in the Arabian peninsula, hunting for game and living upon the spoils of the chase, removed from all the arts of civilization, and it would seem they had become attached to that kind of life. The diet, too, appears to have suited them; for Enos, one of Lehi's grandsons, describes them as early as his day, as a wild, ferocious, blood-thirsty people; full of idolatry and filthiness; feeding upon beasts of prey, and many of them *living upon raw meat.* They lived in tents and wandered about in the wilderness. Their dress consisted of a short skin girdle about their loins, and they shaved their heads. They had become an idle, subtle and mischievous people immediately after landing in the promised land. From being an enlightened, cultivated people, familiar with the arts of life and the knowledge of their race—and the Jewish people of that day still occupied in many respects the foremost rank among the nations—through rejecting the commandments of the Lord, closing their hearts against the Holy Spirit, and indulging in a spirit of murderous hatred against their father and brother, because they chose to serve the Lord, they sank into barbarism, lower even than the Bedouins of the desert in which they had wandered.

Nephi and those who sought for the Spirit of the Lord did not forget, in the midst of the hard life and privations of the wilderness, their former good habits, or throw aside their knowledge of civilization. Their wandering life did not degrade them. Though they had to hunt for the game necessary to sustain them, and, by direction of the Lord, eat its flesh without cooking it, and live in tents, they looked upon that mode of life. not as one that they must follow for ever after, but as necessary only in the providence of the Lord for the time being. Therefore, when they reached the promised land, they became an agricultural and pastoral people of settled habits, living no longer in tents and wandering to and fro, but building houses, establishing cities and turning their attention to mechanism and manufactures and the cultivation of all the arts of true civilization. Of course two branches of a family adopting such dissimilar habits and modes of life would inevitably separate. They would have nothing in common except their origin, and the influence of that would not long remain. The future lives and histories of these two peoples furnish us the most wonderful illustration of the effects of individual example and teachings that we know anything about. Nephi on the one hand and Laman on the other, for good or evil, was each the head and representative man of his family and people. They both had passed through the same outward circumstances. For a wise purpose the Lord had caused them to follow a wandering, and it may be said a wild desert life of eight years. The one had emerged from it stronger, purer, more elevated in thought and action, more attached to those pursuits which make men and nations enlightened, noble and powerful, and more determined when the proper time came to follow them. The other emerged from it a savage in thought, sentiment and practice. He had stifled those human and loving feelings which always exist in the bosoms of men and women who cherish the Spirit of the Lord, and a ferocious, murderous disposition had taken their place. The wild, barbarous life of the desert, with its animal pleasures and excitements of hunting and roving from place to place, with its idleness and filthiness, he became satisfied with, and he never forsook it. He and those who joined him would not have sunk as low as they did had they not been favored, as they had been, in their birth, their surroundings and their opportunities. There was no blessing, favor or power which was possible for man to obtain from the Lord that was not within the reach of Laman, if he had chosen to seek for it. Instead of this, he deliberately, despite every warning, even the words and presence of an angel and the voice of the Lord Himself, rejected everything of the kind and opened his heart to the spirit of hatred and murder. That he did not kill his father and brother was not because of any compunction or lack of effort upon his part. More open and flagrant rebellion against the Lord and everything proceeding from Him, history does not furnish us. Hence his deep fall and the curse which came upon his race. His people and descendants were like him. His wife, children, and all who came within the range of his influence and example, and whom he could persuade, he dragged down with himself. When he died, he bequeathed to his posterity a legacy of unextinguishable hate against everything elevated, noble and good. He chose to be a savage himself, he made his wife and people and descendants savages also. This was Laman, and this the effect of his life, as we glean it from the record embodied in the Book of Mormon.

How great a contrast between his life and that of Nephi! One can scarcely conceive how it would be possible for two men of one family, of the same parentage and brought up under the same circumstances to be more dissimilar. Nephi's constant effort was to lift his people up and to have them exert every power to attain the highest standard of excellence. His example, teachings and labors left an impression upon his people for good, the effect of which was felt for centuries. Still further it can be said with the greatest propriety, that by the revelation of his record, and its translation by the Prophet Joseph, the influence of his teachings and life still operates, and in the years to come will yet exert a mighty power upon the mixed descendants of himself and brothers.

The influence of Laman's life was as potent for evil as Nephi's was for good. We can trace its effects through the ages, widening and deepening as generations came and passed away, casting its baleful shadow upon all who came within its range. No mortal pen can describe the bloodshed, and carnage, and misery which have been the results of his teachings. He imbibed the spirit of falsehood in the outset. He never appears to have done justice to the views and aims of his father and brother. He tortured their teachings and acts, designed for the benefit and happiness of himself and all the company, into causes sufficiently atrocious to justify him in taking their lives. This conception of their characters and motives—and especially so with respect to Nephi—he gave to all who accompanied him. It was indelibly fastened upon the mind of their descendants; and false and cruel as it was, it became the fixed and permanent tradition of their entire race. Though these traditions died out with the disappearance of the Nephites as an organized nationality, there being no longer any reason for keeping them alive, yet we have but to look at the Indians which we see around us, to behold the dreadful consequences of Laman's example, false traditions and life. The wild Indian, as we see him in our day, exactly personifies the life which Laman upwards of twenty-four centuries ago, chose for himself and descendants.

CHAPTER XII.

NEPHI PRACTICALLY THE LEADER—COMMANDED TO BUILD A SHIP—DIRECTED TO THE ORE OUT OF WHICH TO MAKE TOOLS—MAKES A BELLOWS—OBTAINS FIRE—FAULT-FINDING AND RIDICULE OF HIS BRETHREN—HIS SADNESS AND THEIR ELATION—THEY GRUMBLE AT AND REPROACH THEIR FATHER AND HIM—HE REASONS WITH THEM—ENRAGED, THEY ATTEMPT TO THROW HIM IN THE SEA—NEPHI FULL OF POWER OF GOD—THEY DARE NOT TOUCH HIM—THEY ARE SHAKEN BEFORE HIM—FALL DOWN TO WORSHIP HIM—TOLD BY NEPHI TO WORSHIP GOD—NEPHI SHOWN BY THE LORD HOW HE SHOULD WORK TIMBERS, ETC.—NOT WORKED AFTER THE MANNER TAUGHT BY MEN—HELPED BY HIS BROTHERS—SHIP FURNISHED—LAMAN AND OTHERS ACKNOWLEDGE NEPHI'S ABILITY TO BUILD A SHIP—MOUNTAINS AS PLACES OF WORSHIP.

AFTER the colony reached the land Bountiful it is noticeable that the practical leadership devolved upon Nephi, and it continued to be so from that time onward. He had grown strong in body—a stalwart, vigorous, energetic, untiring and undaunted man—but he had also grown in the knowledge and gifts of the Lord. There seemed to be no bounds to his faith. He honored his father, Lehi, and still, doubtless, looked to him for counsel. But Lehi was growing in years and was probably not fitted to take upon him the burden of active labor.

They had now enjoyed a lengthened rest in this charming land; and the time had come for action. It was to Nephi the Lord revealed that which was next to be done. He commanded him to go up into the mountain. When he reached there he cried unto the Lord. The Lord said to him:

"Thou shalt construct a ship, after the manner which I shall show thee, that I may carry the people across the waters."

This was indeed a formidable undertaking for a man with such an experience as he had. He probably knew but little or nothing about ships or their method of construction or the use of tools. But he manifested neither hesitation nor reluctance about undertaking the labor assigned him. He had no doubts of his ability to accomplish it. He knew, as he had expressed himself, that the Lord gave no commandment without preparing the way by which it should be fulfilled; and had He not told him that He would show him in what manner to build it? The Lord directed him to where he could find the ore out of which to make tools. Then Nephi made a bellows with which to blow the fire, out of the skins of beasts. Fire he obtained by striking two stones together. As we have already remarked, the Lord did not suffer them to make much fire as they traveled. He had promised to make their food sweet, so that they would not need to cook it. He had told them also that He would be their light in the wilderness and would prepare the way before them if they would keep His commandments, and they should be led towards the promised land. They were to know that it was by Him they were led. When they should arrive at the promised land, they were to know also that He had brought them out of Jerusalem and had delivered them from destruction.

Nephi had no sooner commenced his labors by obtaining ore out of rock and out of that making tools, and to make his preparations to build a ship, than his brethren began to find fault with and ridicule him. Why, said they, our brother is a

3

fool; he has an idea he can build a ship and also cross this
ocean of waters! They neither believed he could build a ship
nor that he was instructed of the Lord; and they declined to
do any work of that kind. This unbelief and hardness of heart
on their part caused Nephi to be very sorrowful. They noticed
his sadness; but mistook the cause. They supposed it was
because they had discouraged him and he had become convinced he could not build a ship. This idea elated them, and
with an air of triumph they taunted him. We knew, said they,
that you could not construct a ship; for we knew that you did
not have sufficient judgment; you cannot accomplish so great a
work. They reproached him with being like their father, in
being led away by the foolish imaginations of his heart. They
recited their imaginary grievances against Lehi for leading
them out of Jerusalem and bringing upon them the suffering
they and their wives had endured since leaving there.
Warming up with their complaints, they said it would have
been better for their wives to have died before they left Jerusalem than to have had such afflictions as they had borne.
While they were suffering all these hardships in the desert they
might, they said, have been happily enjoying themselves at their
home in Jerusalem. As for the people of Jerusalem, notwithstanding their father's condemnation of them, they declared
they knew them to be a righteous people; for they kept the
statutes and judgments of the Lord, and all His commandments according to the law of Moses. But their father had
led them away, because they had hearkened to him, and now
here was Nephi, their brother, just like their father.

Nephi, according to his custom when they grumbled and
found fault, commenced to reason with and teach them. He
cited to them the history of the children of Israel under the
leadership of Moses, what the Lord had done and the mighty
works He had enabled Moses to do. He did not spare them
in his rebukes. He said they were like the Jews, who had
sought to take his father's life; they also had done the same
thing, and they were murderers, he said, in their hearts, and
they were like the Jews. Said he: "Ye are swift to do
iniquity, but slow to remember the Lord your God." He told
them they had seen an angel and he had spoken unto them.

They had heard the voice of the Lord from time to time; but they were past feeling; they were hard in their hearts. Nephi felt their conduct so acutely that he told them his soul was rent with anguish because of them; and he feared lest they should be cast off for ever. He was so full of the Spirit of the Lord while speaking to them that his frame had no strength.

The only effect his words and remonstrances appeared to have upon them was to enrange them. They went so far as to attempt to throw him into the depths of the sea; but as they advanced towards him for that purpose, he commanded them in the name of the Almighty God not to touch him ; for he was so filled with the power of God, even unto the consuming of his flesh, that whoever should lay his hands upon him should wither even as a dried reed, and he should be as naught before the power of God, for God should smite him. He had so much power on this occasion that they dared not lay their hands upon him or even touch him with their fingers. They dared not do so either for many days. The Spirit of God was so powerful, and it wrought upon them in such a way, that they dared not do this, for fear they should wither before Nephi. In the meantime, Nephi had told them they must murmur no more against their father, and they must not withhold their labor from himself. The Lord had commanded him to build a ship. If he should command him to do all things, he could do them. Even if he should command him to say to that water, be thou earth; if he should say so, it would be done. If the Lord has such power and had wrought so many miracles among the children of men, how is it, he asked, that He could not instruct him how to build a ship? Nephi said many things unto them. The Lord told him to stretch forth his hand again to his brethren, and though they should not wither before him He would shock them, "and this will I do," said the Lord, "that they may know that I am the Lord their God." Nephi did so, and the Lord did shake them, as he had said he would do. This had a great effect upon them. They acknowledged that the Lord was with Nephi and that it was by the power of the Lord they had been shaken; and they fell down before him and were about to worship him; but he would not suffer them. He told them he was their younger brother :

they should worship the Lord their God, and honor their father
and mother, that their days might be long in the land which
the Lord, their God, should give them. Ready to kill him, as
they were at one moment, at another they were ready to
worship him. Strange inconsistency! But there is no con-
sistency about people when they lose the Spirit of God. No
man can tell what he himself will do when he is forsaken by
that Spirit; and no one else can form any idea as to what
vagaries such a person will indulge in, unless it is revealed to
him.

Some manifestation of power was necessary at that time to
subdue these rebellious spirits and bring them into line, so that
they might assist in the work to be done. We presume that
this occurrence made a great impression upon them, and that
they did not shake off very quickly the remembrance of it;
for we are told of no more outbreaks during the building of
the ship. One might think that after such an extraordinary
manifestation of power as they witnessed through Nephi it
would forever cure them of indulging in such a spirit of
rebellion and murder; but, as we shall see as we proceed, it
did not. Their hearts became so impenetrable to all heavenly
influences that the effect upon them of even such a display of
power as they had witnessed and felt upon that occasion, was
not very lasting. They had rejected the Spirit of the Lord,
and had become the servants of that evil one, whom they were
willing to obey; he had power over them and they were led
and prompted by him. Respecting that evil one, the Savior
has said, that he was a liar and a murderer from the beginning,
and he leads all who yield to him to be as he is.

The Lord showed Nephi from time to time how he should
work the timbers of the ship. They were timbers of curious
workmanship, and his brothers helped in this labor. They
were not worked after the manner which was learned by men,
neither was the ship built after their style; but it was built by
Nephi in the manner shown to him by the Lord. It would, of
course, be well adapted for the service required of it. Even
Laman and the rest who shared in his dissatisfaction had to
acknowledge this; for when the ship was finished, and they
saw how suitable it was and how fine the workmanship was,

they had to admit the truth of that which Nephi had told them, that the Lord could teach him how to build a ship; and they humbled themselves before the Lord. While engaged in this labor, Nephi went often to the mountain and prayed unto the Lord, and great things were shown unto him. It is worthy of remark that men of God frequently availed themselves of mountains as places of worship, to which they could go to pray and commune with Him. At such hights and to such men it seems as though the vail between heaven and earth becomes thinner and more easily pierced. The men who have written the most about God, and who have communicated His will to their fellows, have been men who communed with Him in solitary places. By withdrawing to the loneliness of the wilderness or to the mountain top, away from the haunts and tumult of men, they could there obtain the seclusion necessary for the concentration of faith by which they could draw near to and commune with Him undisturbed. Sublime and elevated thoughts are appropriate to such places. In the desert, in the wilderness, and upon mountain peaks, nature is witnessed in all its simple yet impressive majesty, and its solemn stillness is favorable to thanksgiving and prayer, and man is brought nearer to his Creator. The Savior Himself "went up into a mountain apart to pray," and brought His disciples, Peter, James and John "up into a high mountain apart," when He was transfigured and had His interview with Moses and Elias.

CHAPTER XIII.

LEHI COMMANDED TO EMBARK UPON THE SHIP—FOOD PRE-
PARED FOR THE VOYAGE—JACOB AND JOSEPH—DID THE
SHIP HAVE SAILS?—VOYAGES AND SHIPS OF EGYPTIANS
—DANCING AND RUDENESS OF LAMAN AND OTHERS AT
SEA—NEPHI REMONSTRATES—IS TREATED HARSHLY AND
BOUND HAND AND FOOT BY HIS BROTHERS—LEHI AND
SARIAH VERY SICK—FOUR DAYS OF TERRIBLE TEMPEST
—COMPASS WOULD NOT WORK—DRIVEN BACK BEFORE
THE WIND—TERROR OF LAMAN AND LEMUEL—NEPHI'S
PATIENCE AND SELF-CONTROL—THE LORD SHOWS FORTH
HIS POWER—NEPHI RELEASED—THE SHIP STEERED IN
RIGHT COURSE—HIS PRAYER ANSWERED AND TEMPEST
QUELLED—REACH THE PROMISED LAND.

NOW that the vessel was finished, the voice of the Lord
came unto Lehi that they were to embark upon the ship.
It was still through him that the word came for a movement of
this character. They had prepared fruits and meats and honey
in great quantities, and "provisions according to that which the
Lord had commanded them;" these with all their "loading"
and their seeds and everything they had brought with them,
they carried on board their vessel, and embarked themselves,
"every one according to his age." At this point we find
mentioned, for the first time, the names of two sons of Lehi,
who were born in the wilderness—Jacob and Joseph. These
boys grew up to be faithful and renowned men of God, and
were a great help to their brother Nephi, after they reached
the promised land.

After they put forth to sea they were driven by the wind
towards the promised land. We are not informed as to whether
they used sails or other means to propel their vessel; but as
they were "driven before the wind" it is most likely they had

sails.   They steered their ship by the direction of the compass
which the Lord had prepared for them.*

---

*——In this connection it may be of interest to know some-
thing of the progress which had been made in the art of naviga-
tion at the time Lehi and his company made this wonderful
voyage by direction of the Lord.   The earliest record of the
practice of this art after the construction of the ark by Noah—
excepting the account we have in the Book of Mormon of the
voyage of Jared and his brother and their colony—is that of the
Egyptians, who at a very remote period are said to have
established commercial relations with India.   This traffic was
carried on between the Arabian Gulf and the western coast of
India, across the Indian ocean.   It may be that Lehi himself
might have been familiar with a famous expedition by sea which
was fitted out by Necho II. king of Egypt; for as near as we can
ascertain this was done in his day.   This Necho was the king of
Egypt against whom Josiah, king of Judah, fought when he
received his death-wound (*II. Chron. xxxv.* 22).   He fitted out a fleet
in the Red Sea, and having engaged some expert Phœnician pilots
and sailors, he sent them on a voyage of discovery along the coast
of Africa.   They were ordered to start from the Arabian Gulf, and
come round through the Pillars of Hercules (now the straits of
Gibraltar) into the Mediterranean, and so return to Egypt.   This
voyage was a very daring one for those days.   Through it the
peninsular form of Africa was ascertained, and the cape of Good
Hope was doubled about twenty-one centuries before it was seen
by Diaz* or doubled by Vasco de Gama.   The vessels of the
Egyptians were frequently of large dimensions, and were
generally propelled by oars, though they understood to
a certain extent the use of sails.   We read of one vessel in later
times carrying as many as 400 sailors, 4,000 rowers, and nearly
3,000 soldiers.

    There can be no doubt but that the ship upon which Lehi and
his company embarked was in every respect superior for the pur-

---

*——Bartholomew Diaz discovered it in 1487, in the reign of John II., king
of Portugal, but did not land.   He named it Capo Tormento, from the storms
he experienced there; but the king afterwards changed its name to Cape of
Good Hope; and Emanuel, his successor, sent Vasco da Gama, in 1497, with
orders to double it and proceed to India.—*The Ancient Egyptians* (*Wilkinson*)
1, 2, *pp.* 109, 110.

Upon one occasion, after they had been out to sea some time, Laman and Lemuel and the sons of Ishmael and their wives began to dance, to sing and to indulge in very rude language and conduct. They made themselves so merry and behaved so improperly, forgetting by what power they had been brought where they were, that Nephi became alarmed, for fear the Lord would be angry with them and smite them because of their wickedness, and they should go to the bottom of the sea. He spoke to them, therefore, with that soberness and gravity which the sense of peril inspired. But, as usual with them, his words made them angry. They declared that their younger brother should not be a ruler over them. Laman and Lemuel were not content with speaking harshly, they went so far as to handle him roughly and to bind him hand and foot with cords, which were lashed so tightly as to give him pain and to cause his wrists and ankles to be very sore and swollen. They kept him in this condition for four days. It was in vain that his father and mother, his wife and children, and others plead for him. They could not move them to release him. Indeed they threatened every one with vengeance who spoke to them in his favor. This conduct nearly brought Lehi and Sariah down to the gates of death. They became so sick that they were confined to their beds, and were almost ready to be consigned to a watery grave. Yet even this grief and sickness of theirs had no effect upon these cruel and pitiless men. Their hearts were steeled against the voices of love and affection; they were insensible to every humane emotion and every human appeal. Nothing but the power of God could reach them, and they were soon made to feel that. After they had bound Nephi, the compass ceased to work, and they did not know in what direction they should steer the ship. A storm arose, and it

pose for which it was designed to any vessel known among men at that time. The Lord had directed its construction. He knew what was needed—the capacity required, the strain to which it would be subjected from the winds and the waves, and the length of time it would be upon the ocean in making the voyage—and it must have been admirably adapted to meet all these wants.

continued to rage with such violence that they were driven
back, apparently at the mercy of the waves and in great danger
of being engulfed by them. This terrible tempest frightened
Laman and Lemuel exceedingly. They were afraid they and
all on board would be drowned; but they were resolved not to
loose Nephi, even when entreated to do so by their parents and
others. But by the fourth day the tempest had become so fright-
fully fierce, that even Laman and Lemuel were terror-stricken
and softened, and they repented and released Nephi. They had
to be threatened with destruction and brought face to face with
death before they would yield. During all this time, suffering
from pain and in a condition so wretched, Nephi did not lose
his patience and self-control. Great as were his afflictions he
did not murmur against the Lord; but he looked unto Him and
praised Him all the day long. He was in circumstances that
many men would think dreadful and even unbearable: their
faith would be greatly tried thereby, and perhaps would fail.
Our own Church history furnishes a case of this kind. Sidney
Rigdon, once a prominent man in the Church, the first
counsellor of the Prophet Joseph, was taken by the mob in
Missouri at the same time that the prophet and others were,
and was put in prison by them. His afflictions he felt so severely
that he murmured about them, and said:

"I never will follow Brother Joseph's revelations any more,
contrary to my own convenience. The sufferings of Jesus
Christ were a fool to mine."

This doubtless was one cause of his subsequent apostasy; for
he lost the spirit and never afterwards manifested the faith and
power which he had formerly possessed.

The Lord could have manifested His power in behalf of
Nephi so as to have prevented his brothers from binding him
as they did. But it did not suit His purposes to do so. There
are many things which the Lord suffers for the purpose of
testing individuals or the people, and also that He may show
forth His power and to fulfill His word which He has spoken
concerning the wicked. The cruel conduct of Laman and
Lemuel towards Nephi exhibited the wickedness of their hearts
and brought them under condemnation before the Lord, and at
the same time showed up in strong colors his faith and patience

and the greatness of his soul.   After Nephi had been released
he took the compass and it worked as he desired it should, and
he was able to steer the ship in the direction of the promised
land. He prayed unto the Lord and the violence of the tempest
was quelled, and the elements became serene and calm. Sailing
for some time after this occurrence they reached the promised
land.

------ ●◆● ------

CHAPTER XIV.

LAND AND PITCH THEIR TENTS—PLACE OF LANDING—CULTI-
VATE THE GROUND—GOOD CROPS—FIND ANIMALS OF
EVERY KIND—ALSO ORES—RAISE LARGE FLOCKS AND
HERDS—"CARNEROS DE LA TIERRA"—FIND THE HORSE—
WAS THE HORSE EXTINCT WHEN THE WHITES DISCOVERED
AMERICA?—REASONS FOR THINKING IT WAS NOT—WILD
HORSES SEEN BY SIR FRANCIS DRAKE IN 1579—OPINION
OF PROFESSOR MARSH—HORSES SEEN BY DRAKE, NOT
SPANISH.

THEY landed and pitched their tents, and they acknowledged that the Lord had indeed fulfilled His promises
unto them.   He had guided them through the wilderness,
had enabled them to construct a vessel, in which He had
brought them safely across the mighty breadth of ocean which
extended from the coast of Arabia to the coast of what is now
called South America, or as they, with good reason, called it,
"The Promised Land."   The prophet Joseph, in speaking of
their place of landing, said* it was on the coast of the country
now known as Chili—a country which possesses a genial, tem-

---

*——They traveled nearly a south, southeast direction until
they came to the nineteenth degree of north latitude; then,
nearly east to the sea of Arabia, then sailed in a southeast
direction, and landed on the continent of South America, in
Chili, thirty degrees south latitude.

perate and healthy climate. They immediately turned their attention to agriculture. They prepared the ground and put in all the seeds which they had brought with them from the land of Jerusalem. They found the soil admirably adapted for agriculture. Their seeds grew finely and yielded good crops, and they were blessed with abundance. We find no mention made of any seeds being planted by them at any point from the time of their departure from Jerusalem until they reached the promised land. If while encamped in the valley of Lemuel or at Bountiful they cultivated the earth and raised provisions or seeds, we are not informed of it, though doubtless both places were suitable for that purpose.

In exploring the wilderness after their arrival they found animals of every kind—the cow, the ox, the ass and the horse, the goat and the wild goat, and all manner of wild animals which were for the use of man; they also found ores of all kinds, particularly gold, silver and copper. The animals they tamed for their use, and Nephi and his people raised large flocks and herds of animals of every kind. Doubtless they raised herds of a species of camel which is native to the northern part of Chili and to Peru. The Spaniards call them *carneros de la tierra*. These animals in many respects resemble the camel of the old continent; but differ materially in others. They are less in size, but of a more elegant form; they have a small head without horns, but a large tuft of hair adorns the forehead; a very long, slender neck, well proportioned ears, large, round, full, black eyes, a short muzzle, the upper lip more or less cleft; the body is handsomely turned, the legs long and slender, the feet bipartite, or divided in the hoof like the deer and the sheep; the covering of the body is a mixture of hair and wool. The varieties of these animals are the llama, pace, or alpaco, guanaco and vicuna, or vicugna. The size of a full-grown llama is five feet five inches from the bottom of the foot to the top of the shoulders. It is by far the handsomest and most majestic animal of the four. The wool is coarse but so abundant on the body that they carry loads on their backs without pack-saddles. Travelers say that nothing can exceed the beauty of a drove of these animals, as they march along with their cargoes on their backs, each being about a hundred

pounds weight, following each other in the most orderly
manner, equal to a file of soldiers, headed by one with a taste-
fully embroidered halter on his head, covered with small bells,
and a small streamer on his head. Thus they cross the snow-
covered tops of the mountains or defile along their sides.
Many parts of the routes over which they travel are not suitable
for the service of horses or even mules. Like the camel, the
llama kneels to receive its load; but if too heavily laden, it
will refuse to rise until it is lightened. Its wool can only be
used for very ordinary purposes; but that of the alpaco is
manufactured into most beautiful blankets, which are as soft
as silk. Though the llama and the alpaca were domesticated
by the Lamanites before the arrival of the Spaniards in South
America, yet they and the guanaco and the vicuna have never
mixed : the breeds are distinct and will remain so.

Nephi informs us in his record that, among the other
animals which they found in the wilderness upon their arrival
at the promised land, was the horse. There have been persons
who have declared that because of this statement the record
could not be true. They have used this as an argument against
the divine origin of the Book of Mormon ; for, as they have
asserted, the horse was not known upon this continent until it
was brought here by the Spaniards. In this way they have
tried to prove the record to be false. But recent researches by
scientific men have demonstrated beyond the possibility of doubt
that America is the original home of the horse, and at certain
periods it was occupied with horses of many and various forms.
Remains of the true horse as we have it among us at the
present time, have been found all over the land. Professor O.
C. Marsh, whose patient and intelligent investigations have
thrown a flood of light upon this subject, states that the true
horse at one time roamed over the whole of North and
South America. He believes that it became extinct before
the discovery of the continent by Europeans; but, he says, no
satisfactory reason for the extinction has yet been given. In
fact, he acknowledges that at present it is a mystery why the
horse should have been selected for extinction while other
mammals no better adapted than it for the surroundings,
should have survived. He comments freely upon the strange-

ness of its disappearance; for he is evidently convinced that
when the continent was discovered by Europeans it had disappeared, and that we are indebted for our present horse to the
old world, as Europe is called. But we think it is by no means
certain that there were no horses on the continent when it was
discovered by men from Europe.

Robert Dudley, Earl of Northumberland, published a book
"Arcano del Mare," in Florence, Italy, in 1630, (1st, *edition, p.*
46,47) to which Rev. Edward E. Hale referred in a paper read
by him before the American Antiquarian Society (*Proceedings,*
October, 1873, p. 93) in which he states that Sir Francis Drake*
found many wild horses on the west coast of North America,
at which he wondered, because the Spaniards had never found
horses in America. Mr. Hale said:

"The Atlas in the Arcano contains thirty-three maps of
America. My notes on the Munich Atlas show that that contains forty-six maps in manuscript. After the engraved map,
No. 33, the reference to Drake and the coldness of Oregon is
in the following words:

"As the extract from Dudley referred to by Mr. Hale is in
Italian, we give the translation:

"This map is the last of the sixth book which [map] begins
with the port of New Albion [Nuovo Albion]—longitude 237°

---

*——Sir Francis Drake was engaged in his celebrated voyage
round the world. His fleet consisted of three vessels—the
Pelican, of one hundred tons, the *Elizabeth* and the *Marigold,*
each of eighty. He entered the Pacific ocean from the straits of
Magellan, on the 6th of September, 1578. On the 30th he lost
sight of the *Marigold* in a gale, and never saw her again. On
the 16th of April, 1579, he left the port of Guatulco, on the Mexi-
can coast, and having sailed west and afterwards north, he ran
as far north as the parallel of 43°, or, according to other accounts,
of 48° north latitude. Bryant, in his Popular History of the
United States, (vol. 2, p. 577) says that Humboldt evidently
thought that Drake sailed that far north (*see Humboldt's "New*
Spain," ii. 337 et seg.) as this latitude corresponds best of all with
the severe cold. Opinions vary as to whether the port which
Drake called New Albion was the bay of San Francisco or not;
but the evidence is that it was.

and latitude 38°— discovered by the Englishman, Drake, about 1579, as [said] above, a place favorable for taking in water and getting other necessaries. The said Drake found that the savages of the country were very courteous and kind, and the land pretty fruitful, and the air temperate. He saw rabbits in great numbers, but with tails as long as [those of] rats, and [saw] *many wild horses, with the more wonder because the Spaniards never saw horses in America* (e [*vidde*] *di molti cavalli saluatichi, con maggiore maraviglia, atteso chegli pagnuoli non viddero mai cavalli nell' America*); and the reason that Drake sought and found the said port was this,— that having passed the true cape Mendozino,—latitude 42°. 30′—to take water, at 43° 30′ north latitude he found the coast so cold in the month of June, that his crew could not bear it;—at which he quite wondered, the latitude being about the same as that of Tuscany, and of Rome in Italy."

In a conversation with Professor Marsh, at Washington, in the winter of 1881, we called his attention to this statement of Dudley's. He had heard of it; but, possessed of the belief that the horse was extinct when Europeans came to this continent, he was not inclined to accept Dudley's statement as true. Yet, aside from the wide-spread and generally accepted belief that there were no horses on the continent at the time of its discovery, there is no evidence which has come to the knowledge of paleontologists or naturalists to prove that the horse was not here at that time. The evidence of its existence up to a comparatively recent period are abundant all over the continent, and wonder is expressed by investigators that it should have disappeared. But did it disappear? Six hundred years before the advent of the Savior, Lehi and his company found the horse in South America. There is no reason to doubt that it was preserved by his descendants up to the time of the extinction of the Nephites, early in the fifth century of our era It is customary to account for the immense herds of American horses on the assumption that the Spaniards introduced them. But if Drake and his companions saw these horses as described by Dudley, they could not have been descendants of Spanish horses; for no Spaniards had penetrated that country or been within hundreds of miles of it at the time

of its discovery by Drake, in 1579. Viceroy Mendoza, who
succeeded Cortez, by appointment of the Emperor Charles, in
the civil administration of the Spanish possessions, Cortez
being restricted to his duties as military commander, sent out
Vasquez de Coronado to find the seven cities of Cibola, of the
wealth of which the Spaniards had heard very wonderful
stories. As early as 1540 he penetrated the country as far as
the territory now know as New Mexico and probably into
Arizona. He and his troop had horses; but even if they had
lost or turned loose any, it is most improbable that in thirty-
nine years they would have multiplied into large herds observed
by Drake on the sea board, which as we know was at least five
hundred miles away. Coronado had but few horses, would
have had fewer brood mares, and would have been apt to mention any loss of a large number of auxiliaries so essential to
his expedition. Dudley published his work in Italy, where
he was residing, in, 1630. He was a navigator himself, and was
the son-in-law of Cavendish, one of the explorers of the South
seas. He was well acquainted with the survivors of Drake's
voyages. His description of the wild horses they saw has
nothing improbable about it; for until quite recently wild
horses roamed in herds over all that country. At the time we
settled in this territory wild horses in California were very
numerous. And we see no reasons to doubt the correctness of
Dudley's statement that Drake saw them in great numbers
when he visited the coast in 1579.

CHAPTER XV.

ANIMALS AND VEGETABLES VALUABLE TO LEHI AND COM-
PANY—THE POTATO—ABUNDANCE OF FRUITS—JERUSALEM
DESTROYED—LEHI'S THANKFULNESS FOR THIS CHOICE
LAND—A LAND OF LIBERTY TO ALL WHO SHOULD BE
BROUGHT HERE IF THEY WOULD SERVE GOD—LAND TO BE
KEPT FROM KNOWLEDGE OF OTHER NATIONS—REMARK-
ABLY FULFILLED—PROMISES OF THE LORD TO LEHI
CONCERNING HIS DESCENDANTS AND THE LAND—PRESENT
CONDITION OF HIS SEED PREDICTED—PROPHECIES CON-
CERNING THE PROPHET JOSEPH SMITH—LEHI A
GREAT PROPHET—RESTRAINS HIS CHILDREN WHILE
LIVING—RANCOROUS HATRED AFTER HIS DEATH AGAINST
NEPHI—ENRAGED BY HIS ADMONITIONS—PROPOSE TO
KILL HIM.

THE animals of the country Lehi, and his company doubtless found of very great value to them in their labors and
movements.   Besides these, it is probable they obtained many
valuable vegetable productions which were peculiar to the
country.   The potato is indigenous to that region; it seems to
be its natural home, and was found growing there in abundance
by the first Europeans that visited the country.   It is not
unlikely that Lehi and his people also had it for use.   Wild
fruits are now very abundant in places contiguous to the spot
were we are told they landed.   One writer, in describing a contiguous province, says :

"The wild Indians bring from the woods many delicious
fruits, pine-apples, plantains, bananas, nisperos, mamays,
guavas, etc., as well as sweet potatoes, *camotes*, cabbage palm,
palmitos, and yucas."

If Lehi and his company found wild fruits so abundant, they
had no difficulty in living in plentiful ease until the seed grains
they brought with them matured.   Everything contributed to
make them feel that it was a choice land above all other lands;

for with all the other advantages it possessed, the soil was exceedingly fertile and the climate was delicious in temperature and healthy. Shortly after their arrival, Lehi informed his people that he had learned through a vision from the Lord that Jerusalem had been destroyed, and he said had they remained there, they also would have perished. He drew the attention of his children to the goodness of the Lord in warning them to flee out of Jerusalem and in preserving them until they had reached this choice land, which the Lord had covenanted should be for the inheritance of his seed forever, and also for all those who should be led out of other countries by the hand of the Lord. To those brought out of other countries this should be a land of liberty, so long as they should serve God according to the commandments which He has given; but if iniquity should abound the land should be cursed for their sakes. He told them that this land would be kept from the knowledge of other nations; for the reason that, if they discovered it, they would overrun it and there would be no place for an inheritance.

This explains why the world remained so long in ignorance of this continent. It was hidden from the world, and was almost a world by itself for centuries, its people having no communication with any other nation upon the earth. Generation succeeded generation, numerous and large cities were built, the whole land was covered with people, the arts of a high civilization were cultivated, revolutions, wars and great changes were effected and all the busy scenes of human life were enacted upon this continent, and yet the inhabitants of other lands were as ignorant of its existence as if it had belonged to another planet. This ignorance continued until the Lord moved upon Christopher Columbus to penetrate the great ocean which stretched between it and Europe. Men called it "the new world," and it was a new world to them; and though the evidences that highly-cultivated races had occupied the land for ages are abundant upon every hand, those who do not believe the Book of Mormon are still as ignorant of who they were, or where they came from and of all their history, excepting those facts which have been brought to light by the examination of the ruins of their cities, as they were when the continent was brought to the knowledge of the world.

3*

Lehi gives the true explanation of the reason why this continent should be concealed from the knowledge of other nations. We see how it is to-day. This continent is so desirable that there is a steady stream of people flowing to it from all countries. They are filling up the land, and the Lamanites, who have occupied it under the promise of the Lord to their father Lehi, have been crowded back from both oceans until they have but small spots to live upon in the center of the land, and even these are coveted by the people of other nations who have come here. This would have been the result long, long ago had the world known of the existence of this continent; but the Lord concealed it, and guided those only to it whom He desired to occupy it, so that all His promises concerning it might be fulfilled. Lehi told his children, that if those whom the Lord should bring out of the land of Jerusalem should keep His commandments, they should not only prosper here, but they should be kept from all other nations and have the land to themselves; there should be none to molest them, nor to take the land away from them; but they should dwell safely for ever. It was the failure of the ancestors of the Indians, or Lamanites, to do this, that brought upon them and their children evils under which they at present suffer. Lehi, before his death, told them, by the spirit of prophecy, what their fate would be if they fell into unbelief and rejected the Lord. He said the Lord would bring other nations unto them, and He would give them power; they would take away from his descendants their lands, and they would be scattered and smitten. We have only to look around us to see how completely and exactly his predictions have been fulfilled. And as these predictions have come to pass, so will others also come to pass respecting the nations of the Gentiles that will occupy this land: they would not be permitted to utterly destroy the descendants of Nephi or the other children of Lehi; and if they, themselves, did not repent, and keep the commandments of the Lord, destruction would also fall upon them.

Among other plain and definite predictions which Lehi made unto his children was one respecting the birth and mission of the Prophet Joseph Smith. He quoted from a prophecy of Joseph, the son of Jacob, who was sold into Egypt, to the effect that "a seer shall the Lord my God raise up, who shall be a choice seer unto the fruit of my loins." His name was foretold. He was to be called after the Patriarch Joseph and after his own father. The predictions of Lehi which he gave to his children before his death are very precious, because of their covering so many points and being so plain. He was a great prophet; the Lord had revealed to him a wonderful amount of knowledge concerning the future; and he was especially favored in having such a land as this given, by covenant of the Lord, as an inheritance to himself and his posterity. He did all in his power to teach his children and his people the ways of the Lord and to make them in some degree worthy of the favor which had been shown unto them; but with Laman and Lemuel and those who associated with them his tender entreaties, his solemn warnings, his severe rebukes, and his inspired and pointed predictions were all of no avail. They had gone from bad to worse until their hearts had become like flint, and no good impression could be made upon them. They were full of malice and the spirit of murder. While he lived, his presence had some restraining effect upon them. He was still the father and head of the people, whose authority and counsel, though often disregarded by his rebellious offspring, could not be altogether set aside. But he was scarcely buried before the rancorous hatred of Laman and Lemuel and their adherents broke out against Nephi. It was his admonitions concerning their iniquities that enraged them. His rebukes, they said, afflicted them; they viewed them as an attempt upon his part to dictate and rule over them. He was their younger brother, and they declared they would not have him as a ruler; for this right belonged to them, they said, as the seniors. They proposed to kill him. This brought affairs to a crisis.

CHAPTER XVI.

NEPHI'S EFFORTS TO SAVE HIS BRETHREN—NEPHI, COM-
MANDED OF THE LORD, FLEES INTO THE WILDERNESS—
HIS COMPANY—HIS SISTERS—CARRIES PLATES OF BRASS
AND OTHER RECORDS—THE LIAHONA AND SWORD OF
LABAN WITH HIM—NEPHI CALLED A LIAR AND A ROBBER
—SEARCHES THE SCRIPTURES—TWO SETS OF PLATES—
CHARACTER OF RECORDS ON EACH—PLATES MADE FOR
A SPECIAL PURPOSE—FOUND BY MORMON—WISDOM OF
GOD GREATER THAN CUNNING OF DEVIL—THE PROPHET
JOSEPH DELIVERED FROM A SNARE.

FOR many years Nephi had done all in his power to sustain the influence of his father with his brothers. In company with his father he had labored steadily to induce them to live righteously and to obey the commandments of God. He had exhausted every means to induce them to dwell in union, peace and love. There was nothing more he could do, except to become a victim to their blind and cruel rage. But this, in the providence of the Lord, was not required of him. The Lord had another work for Nephi, so He warned him to flee into the wilderness, and leave his wicked brothers and associates to themselves. Those who accompanied Nephi in this flight were all who believed in the warnings and revelations of God. They accepted the word of the Lord as it came to him concerning this departure. The record informs us that they were his own family, Zoram and his family, Sam and his family, his brothers Jacob and Joseph and his sisters and others. The names of his sisters are not given, and we are not told how many there were, or who the others were who accompanied him. With their tents and everything which it was possible for them to carry, they took their journey into the wilderness. Nephi was careful to have all the records of his people with him. He had the plates of brass which were obtained from Laban, and his father, and his father Lehi's record, and the records he had kept himself, and also the ball or compass, which was prepared of the Lord for Lehi, and the sword of Laban.

We are not informed what the feelings of Laman and Lemuel were respecting Nephi's keeping possession of the brass plates, the record of Lehi and the ball or compass which the Lord had prepared for Lehi; but it is not too much to suppose that while they kept no records themselves upon plates, and therefore placed no value upon them, they were angry at Nephi for taking these with him. They probably accused him of robbing them; for, about five centuries after this, we find (Alma xx. 13) that the tradition among their descendants was that Nephi was not only a liar, but had robbed their fathers. Nephi, himself, was very particular about keeping records. He taught his people to value the written word. He doubtless devised means of giving them copies of that which had been written, for in the days of his brother Jacob the sudden and awful death of a teacher of false doctrine who had led many astray, caused the people, as we are told (Jacob vii. 23), to search the scriptures. We conclude from this that copies of the writings upon the brass plates must have been accessible to them.

By the command of the Lord, Nephi made two sets of plates, on which to keep the records of his people. The first set of these plates contained in great fullness and detail the history of the people of Nephi. Upon them Nephi engraved the record of his father Lehi, and the genealogy of Lehi, his prophecies and many of his own prophecies and the most part of all their proceedings in the wilderness. Upon them were engraved by him with more detail and particularity the things which transpired before he made the second set of plates. Upon these first plates also an account was given of the wars, contentions and destructions of the people, during Nephi's lifetime, and he commanded his people that they should continue to do this after he was gone, including an account of the reign of the kings, and that the plates should be handed down from one generation to another, or from one prophet to another, until the Lord should command otherwise.

It was from these plates, called the plates of Nephi, that the Prophet Mormon made his abridgment which the Prophet Joseph first translated. It will be remembered that while the prophet was translating the Book of Mormon he was teased by Martin Harris to let him have some of the manuscript. Joseph did so. The Lord was so displeased with him for letting these writings go out of his hands, that he deprived him of his gift, and the work of translating was suspended for a number of months. While in Martin Harris' possession, the manuscripts were stolen and were not recovered. Those who obtained them had a deep design in view. But the Lord thwarted them. He gave Joseph a commandment not to attempt to translate a second time that which he had lost, but to translate the record which he would find upon the second set of plates, called also the plates of Nephi. The revelation respecting this is to be found in the Book of Doctrine and Covenants, section x.

Nephi informs us that he had been commanded of the Lord to make these second plates for a special and wise purpose; but he did not know what that purpose was, farther than there should be an account engraved thereon of the ministry of his people and the more plain and precious parts of the prophecies, so that they might be kept for the instruction of his people. These plates were handed down from Nephi to Amaleki, covering a period of about four hundred years from the time that Lehi left Jerusalem. When Amaleki finished his writing, the plates, which were small, were full; and as he had no children, he gave them to the king, whose name was Benjamin. This king kept them with the other, and larger plates of Nephi, which contained the record of kings, and which had been handed down from generation to generation. They were kept from that time forth with the other records upon plates, which in the lapse of centuries became very numerous, until they came into the hands of the Prophet Mormon. Mormon made his abridgment sometime after the year 384 of the Christian era, which was upwards of five centuries after the death of this King Benjamin. After he had made his abridgment from the large plates of Nephi, down to the days of King Benjamin, he found, in searching among the records, these small plates of Nephi. Their contents pleased him. They were full of revelations, and prophecies concerning the coming of Christ and many other great events. He knew that many events therein predicted had been fulfilled, and also that those predictions

which went beyond his day would most assuredly come to pass;
therefore, they were precious to him, and he knew they would
be also to posterity. But, in addition to these reasons for
selecting them, he was moved upon by the Spirit of the Lord
to embody them with his record. The promptings of the
Spirit to him were that there was a wise purpose in this, though
it does not appear that he fully knew what that purpose was.
But the purpose became plain when the Lord gave again to the
Prophet Joseph the gift and privilege of translating. He was
commanded to translate the record engraved upon these plates, to
supply the place of that translation which had been stolen. Thus
Joseph was told not to translate over again that which he had
translated, and Satan's plan to entrap him was defeated. For
the Lord, foreseeing what would take place, had inspired Nephi
and Mormon to do as they did; the one to prepare the plates
and engrave upon them and to command those who followed
him to do so also; and the other to embody them with his
record to afterwards come into the hands of the Prophet
Joseph; and the results are that we have in the Book of
Mormon a body of revelations and prophecies that are exceedingly precious and which throw a flood of light upon the doctrines of Christ and those mighty events which are to take
place in the last days.

CHAPTER XVII.

TRAVEL MANY DAYS IN THE WILDERNESS—CALL THE
LAND NEPHI—DID THEY JOURNEY NORTHWARD?
LOCATION OF LAND NEPHI—RIVER SIDON AND MAGDA-
LENA—LAND OF ZARAHEMLA—TWENTY-TWO DAYS' TRAVEL
FROM NEPHI—DID NOT LAND OF NEPHI EXTEND
CONSIDERABLY SOUTH?—ZENIFF'S RETURN TO THE LAND
OF NEPHI—WAS THAT THE LAND SETTLED BY NEPHI,
THE FIRST?—MOSIAH, KING OF ZARAHEMLA—REASONS
FOR THINKING NEPHI TO BE DISTINGUISHING NAME OF
AN EXTENSIVE REGION—NEPHITES WOULD SPREAD
OVER THE COUNTRY IN FOUR HUNDRED YEARS—DID
NEPHI AND COMPANY TRAVEL AS FAR NORTH AS ECUA-
DOR?—FOLLOWED BY LAMANITES—JACOB AND ENOS
RESPECTING LAMANITES—NEPHI'S DESCRIPTION OF THE
LAND—BOLIVIA AND PERU—CITIES AND SETTLEMENTS
CALLED AFTER FOUNDERS—ADDITIONAL REASONS FOR
THINKING NEPHI AND COMPANY DID NOT SETTLE SO
FAR NORTH—BOUNDARIES OF LANDS OCCUPIED BY
NEPHITES AND LAMANITES—SOUTH AMERICA CALLED
LEHI, NORTH AMERICA CALLED MULEK.

AFTER they separated from Laman and Lemuel, Nephi
and his company traveled for many days in the wilderness and reached a land where they determined to settle. They
selected for it the name of their leader, and it was called
Nephi.

Nephi does not state in what direction he and his company
traveled after separating from his brethren; but it is plain,
from the allusions which are subsequently made to this land of
Nephi by other writers, that they took their journey northward. It appears plain also that they traveled some distance
in that direction. As Nephi was always careful to seek the
guidance of the Lord in his movements, he was undoubtedly led
by Him to the land where they settled. It is stated by Elder

Orson Pratt, in a foot-note to the new edition of the Book of Mormon, that the land of Nephi is supposed to have been in or near the country now called Ecuador. This supposition is based upon the general understanding that the river called the Sidon in the Book of Mormon is that now known as the Magdalena in our geographies. If this is correct, we can locate the land of Zarahemla with tolerable accuracy from the references which are made to it in the Book of Mormon; and as journeys were made between those two lands—Nephi and Zarahemla—and in one instance the time occupied in the journey is given —about twenty-two days—(Mosiah xxiii. 4, xxiv 20-25,) some idea can be obtained of the distance between these two places.

But there are reasons for thinking that the land called Nephi was an extensive region, and that it reached much farther south than the country now known as Ecuador. Nearly four centuries after Nephi and his company separated from Laman and Lemuel and their companions, a prophet by the name of Mosiah was warned by the Lord to flee out of the land of Nephi, and to take with him all the Nephites who would "hearken unto the voice of the Lord." They were led by the power of God, through the wilderness, to the land of Zarahemla. Afterwards, some of the children of those who thus fled had a desire to return to the old home of their fathers, and expeditions were fitted out for that purpose. One of them under Zeniff was successful in securing a foothold in that land, though it had by that time been taken possession of by the Lamanites. By treaty with the king of the Lamanites, Zeniff and his people were permitted to occupy the cities of Lehi-Nephi and Shilom and the contiguous lands. They erected buildings and repaired the walls of those cities and cultivated the ground. Zeniff became their king. His son Noah succeeded him. In his days, Alma, a descendant of Nephi, baptized a number of people and organized them into a church. Being persecuted by King Noah, they left that country, and after meeting various adventures, reached Zarahemla. They numbered, when they started, four hundred and fifty souls. and we learn that the journey occupied about twenty-two days. This leads to the conclusion that the city of Lehi-Nephi, from which they started, could not have been farther south than the country now called Ecuador.

But the inquiry arises, was this the place to which Nephi led his company when they separated from Laman and Lemuel and their adherents? The record informs us that when they fled from their wicked brethren they journeyed for many days, and they pitched their tents, "and," Nephi says, "my people would that we should call the name of the place Nephi; wherefore we did call it Nephi." Nearly four hundred years after this we find in the book of Omni (i. 12):

"Behold, I will speak unto you somewhat concerning Mosiah, who was made king over the land of Zarahemla: for behold, he being warned of the Lord that he should flee out of the land of Nephi, and as many as would hearken unto the voice of the Lord, should also depart out of the land with him, into the wilderness."

It appears clear that this name of Nephi was a general name for a large region of country, which comprised within its borders many smaller divisions known by various names. We infer this from the record; for Zeniff, upon his return to that which he calls, "the land of our fathers," had the liberty given him to occupy two places, or divisions, which he calls, "the land of Lehi-Nephi and the land of Shilom." Adjoining these was a portion of country known as "the land of Shemlon," which the Lamanites retained in their possession. In the borders of the country occupied by Zeniff and his Nephite people, was a place called Mormon. It was after this place that the great prophet and general of the Nephite nation, who led the hosts in the last, great conflict, was called. He himself speaks of it (III. Nephi v. 12) as "the land of Mormon." So it appears plain that there were many local divisions in the region which the Nephites had occupied.

We see that those whom Nephi led away from his wicked brethren, called the first place where they settled Nephi and themselves Nephites. Would not the same reasons prompt the nation as it increased and spread over the land, to call the whole region which it occupied, embracing all its local divisions, Nephi, or the land of Nephi, as its great distinguishing name? From the point where Nephi first settled, it is quite likely his people extended to the northward; for in that direction they had room to spread, without coming in contact with the Lamanites. In this way the limits of "the land of Nephi" would be enlarged. Our own history in these mountains shows how this would be done. The Latter-day Saints came to the land we now call Utah thirty-four years ago. Salt Lake City was then settled. Since 1847 we have spread over a large extent of country. But this is a brief space, compared with the centuries which elapsed from the time that Nephi and his company fled from his brethren, to the departure of Mosiah and his company into the wilderness when they found Zarahemla. Though in the beginning the Nephites were but few in number, it is easy to understand that, in the space of nearly four hundred years, they would become quite numerous. We are told, that when two hundred years had elapsed they "had waxed strong in the land," as were also the Lamanites. Were not the cities of Lehi-Nephi and Shilom, and the lands bearing those names, some of the most northern of the Nephite settlements? There was a country, stretching to the south of those cities and lands, known by the general name of Nephi, which they had occupied, and from which they, doubtless, receded, through the pressure of the Lamanites upon them from the south, during the long period of time concerning which we have such brief mention. We know that the place where Lehi and his people landed on the continent was in the 30° of south latitude. Between this point and the southern boundary of Ecuador is a space of 26° of latitude, and includes the choice and desirable countries now known as the northern part of Chili, and Bolivia, and Peru—countries admirably adapted for the settlement and defense of a people like the Nephites. The question arises: Did Nephi and his people traverse this great distance when he separated himself from his brethren?

When Nephi and his people fled, they were followed, before long, by the Lamanites; for it appears that it was but a short period until Nephi manufactured swords, after the fashion of the sword of Laban, for his people to use in defending themselves against the attacks of the Lamanites. When forty years

had elapsed, Nephi informs us there had been wars and contentions between the two peoples; and Jacob, in speaking of his
brother Nephi, and that which he had done for his people and
their love for him, says that he had "wielded the sword of
Laban in their defense." Jacob, and Enos, his son, speak of
the Lamanites in such a manner as to leave no doubt that they
and the whole Nephite people were familiar with them and
their modes of life, and that they tried to teach them (Jacob ii.
35; iii. 5-9; Enos i. 13, 14, 20.). Whatever the distance, therefore, may have been that Nephi and his company fled, the
Lamanites must have made the same journey not long after.
Nephi informs us that they journeyed in the wilderness "for
the space of many days" before they reached the place they
called after his own name. His description of it leaves no
doubt as to its fertility, its advantage for grazing, its abundance
of timber, and its great mineral wealth. Besides the common
metals, he speaks of gold and silver, and other precious ores,
as being in great abundance. Traveling as they did, a company of men, women and children, with tents and other baggage, it would have required a journey of very "many days"
from their place of landing to get beyond the confines of what
is now called Chili and into Bolivia. In the lands now known
as Bolivia and Peru, places can be found, which correspond
exactly with the description of the place of settlement given
in the record, particularly in the abundance of the precious
metals. Those countries have not been excelled, even in our
day, in the yield of these ores by any country in the world.
Some of their mines are world-renowned; and within their borders places of great natural strength, which could be easily
fortified against the incursions of a savage foe, are very numerous. Commencing their settlements here, and calling the land
Nephi and themselves Nephites, they whom Nephi led could
spread to the northward as they increased and necessity required
still applying the general name of Nephi to the whole country,
but distinguishing their cities and settlements and sub-divisions
by the names of their founders, as was their custom (Alma viii.
7), or by other names that circumstances might suggest, until
they reached, in the days of Mosiah, as far north as what is
now known as Ecuador, and had cities there, near the wilder-

ness on the north, known as Nephi or Lehi-Nephi, Shilom, Shemlon, etc.

Another reason also causes this view to appear probable; Nephi and his company could scarcely have settled at a point twenty-two days journey from Zarahemla without their descendants—scattered as they were upon the face of the land —coming in contact with the Zarahemlaites at an earlier date than the days of Mosiah, even though the people of Zarahemla may not have long resided at the point where he found them. It does not appear probable that, if the city of Nephi, or Lehi-Nephi as it is sometimes called, had been the city founded by the first Nephi, there would have been a wilderness so close to it on the north, as there appears from the record to have been, after four hundred years had elapsed.

In the description of the boundaries of the lands occupied by the Nephites and the Lamanites (Alma xxii. 27-32) it is stated that, "the more idle part of the Lamanites lived in the wilderness, and dwelt in tents; and they were spread through the wilderness, on the west, in the land of Nephi; yea, and also on the west of the land of Zarahemla, in the borders by the seas-hore, and on the west, in the land of Nephi, in the place of their fathers' first inheritance, and thus bordering along by the sea-shore."

Here our two allusions to the land of Nephi, and without desiring to favor any particular theory or to strain the language to sustain any special views, it conveys to us the idea, when taken in connection with other facts contained in the record, that the land of Nephi was, as we have said, an extensive region, embracing at least the west side of the continent with the Pacific shore for some distance to the south, and perhaps embracing within its boundaries the whole of the south continent outside of the limits of Zarahemla. In the same chapter (verse 34) the same idea is clearly expressed in the language "that the Lamanites could have no more possessions only in the land of Nephi and the wilderness round about," and this, too, at a time when the whole continent, south of the line of the land of Zarahemla, was either in possession of the Lamanites, or open to them. It must not be forgotten, however, that what is now known in geography as South America was

called Lehi, and North America was called Mulek by the
Nephites. (Helaman vi. 10).

---◆---

CHAPTER XVIII.

TRAVELERS' DESCRIPTIONS OF LAND ONCE OCCUPIED BY
NEPHITES—CRADLE OF AN IMPERIAL RACE—THE PRO-
DUCTIONS OF THE LAND IN MODERN TIMES AGREE WITH
DESCRIPTION OF SAME IN BOOK OF MORMON—RAPID
RECOVERY FROM EFFECTS OF DISASTROUS COMMOTIONS
AND WARS ACCOUNTED FOR—HEALTHY CLIMATE—
REMARKABLE LONGEVITY—JACOB, ENOS, JAROM AND
OMNI—LONGEVITY OF INDIANS IN ECUADOR AND PERU.

A TRAVELER by the name of Markham, (Jour. of English Geog. Soc. Vol. xli., 1871, pp. 285, 286.) in speaking
of the country between the northern line of Chili and the
southern line of Ecuador—the country which we think was
called the land of Nephi, and in some portion of which Nephi
settled with his people when he fled from his brethren—says:

"This vast tract comprises every variety of climate, and contains within its limits most prolific tropical forests, valleys with
the climate of Italy, a coast region resembling Sinde or Egypt,
temperate hillsides or plateaux, bleak and chilling pasture
lands, and lofty peaks and ridges within the limits of eternal
snows. On one mountain side the eye may embrace, at a single
glance, sugar cane and bananas under cultivation in the lowest
zone, waving fields of Indian corn a little higher up, shaded
by tall trees, orchards of tropical fruits, stretches of wheat and
barley, steep slopes, covered with potatoes and quinua, bleak
pastures where llamas and alpacas are browsing, and rocky
pinnacles streaked with snow."

Such a country, with such a variety of climates and products,
was well adapted for the cradle of an imperial race as the
Nephites proved to be. The mighty obstacles of nature, which

some portions of that country presented, were such as to tax their ingenuity to the utmost. But Humboldt has well observed that,

"When enterprising races inhabit a land where the form of the ground presents to them difficulties on a grand scale which they may conquer and overcome, the contest with nature becomes a means of increasing their strength and power as well as their courage."

Stevenson, in his "Twenty Years in South America," says, in speaking of one of the provinces of this region:

"The various climates, assisted by the various localities of the soil, would produce all the necessaries and all the luxuries of life; for in the small compass of fifty leagues, a traveler experiences the almost unbearable heat of the torrid zone, the mild climates of the temperate, and the freezing cold of the polar regions."

The cities of Lehi-Nephi and Shilom, which Zeniff calls "the land of our fathers," were, doubtless, delightfully situated and possessed every advantage of climate and soil. This appears evident from the anxiety of some of the children of those whom Mosiah, by the command of the Lord, led away from that land through the wilderness to Zarahemla, to go back there and live. Modern travelers speak in language of the highest praise of the region in some part of which we suppose those cities stood. Spruce, an English traveler, (Jour. of English Geog. Soc., Vol. xxxi., 1861, p. 175) says, in speaking of the plains in Ecuador:

"A journey of four hours will place the traveler in the region of eternal frost, or, in the space of half a day, he can descend the deep and sultry valleys that separate the mighty chain of the Andes; or, finally, he may visit the tropical forest extending to the shores of the Pacific. This variation of temperature, dependent on elevation, and occurring within narrow limits, furnishes a daily and diversified supply of vegetable food: from the plantain. which as a substitute for bread, is largely consumed by the inhabitants of the coast, to the wheat, potato and other grains and roots, growing luxuriantly on the cool table-lands of the interior. Besides these, the market is furnished with pine-apples, chirunoyas (*anour chi-*

runoya) guayavas (*pridium promiferum*) guavas (*ingapachy-carpa*), the fruits of different species of passion-flower, oranges and lemons; and, from January to April, certain European fruits, such as apples, pears, quinces, peaches, apricots, and strawberries."

Stevenson says of a part of this region which he visited:

"These valleys are principally under cultivation, and bless the husbandman with a continued succession of crops; for the uninterrupted sameness of the climate in any spot is such as to preclude the plant as well as the fruit from being damaged by sudden changes in the temperature of the atmosphere, changes which are in other countries so detrimental to the health of the vegetable world. The fertility of some of these valleys exceeds all credibility, and the veracity of the description would be doubted, did not the knowledge of their localities and the universal description of the equability and benignity of these climates ensure the probability. An European is astonished on his first arrival here to see the plough and the sickle, the sower and the thrashing-floor, at the same time in equal requisition: to see at one step an herb fading through age, and at the next, one of the same kind springing up—one flower decayed and drooping and its sisters unfolding their beauties to the sun —some fruits inviting the hand to pluck them, and others in succession beginning to show their ripeness—others can scarcely be distinguished from the color of the leaves which shade them, while the opening blossoms, insure a continuation. Nothing can be more beautiful than to stand on an eminence and observe the different gradations of the vegetable world, from the half unfolded blade just springing from the earth, to the ripe harvest yellowing in the sun and gently waving in the breeze. An enumeration of the different vegetable productions of this province would be useless; it will be sufficient to observe, that grain, pulse, fruits, esculents and horticultural vegetables are produced in the greatest abundance and of an excellent quality, as well as all kinds of flesh meat and poultry."

Another traveler, Hassaurck, who resided four years in that country as United States minister, gives us an equally enchanting description of portions of Ecuador which he visited.

Speaking of the country around Cotodachi and Hatuntaqui, he says, it "is chiefly a grain region. Indian-corn, barley, wheat, and potatoes grow in unlimited abundance. All the grains and fruits of the temperate zone could be introduced here. In the gardens and orchards, the peach, the fig-tree and the wild grape grow by the side of the chirimoya, the aquacate, and the raspberry. The climate is delightful. It is the same all the year round: no torrid season enervates the inhabitants of this favored realm; no icy winter sends him shivering to the chimney fire. In fact, stoves and chimneys are unknown; and to know what heat is, one would have to descend to the sultry valley of the Chota, where the negro hums his merry tunes among coffee and plantain trees and the sugar cane. There is no starvation in this neighborhood; nobody dies from cold; nobody sinks sunstruck to the ground; no troublesome insects molest the inhabitants; epidemics are unknown; healthy faces peep at you through the long hedges of aloes; healthy faces stare at you from every Indian cottage. It is not sickness, it is foreign war and internecine strife and perpetual convulsions, that decimate the population and scatter death and decay where wealth and bliss should smile.

> "The golden harvests spring; the unfailing sun
> Sheds light and life; the fruits, the flowers, the trees,
> Arise in due succession; all things speak
> Peace, and harmony, and love. The universe,
> In Nature's silent eloquence, declares
> That all fulfill the works of love and joy.
> All but the outcast man! He fabricates
> The sword which stabs his peace; he cherisheth
> The snakes that gnaw his heart."

The description of Ecuador, its climate and its productions, by modern travelers agrees with that which is said in the Book of Mormon concerning the lands of Lehi-Nephi and of Shilom, which Zeniff and his company entered into treaty with the king of the Lamanites to re-possess. They raised all manner of seeds—corn, wheat, barley, neas and sheum—and all kinds of fruits. From this brief description by Zeniff of the productions of the land we can gather a very correct idea of the character of the climate and the soil. The climate was not too hot for wheat and barley, nor too cool for all kinds of fruits; in fact if not exactly the same land as that visited by the modern travelers from whom we quote, it was a land resembling it in climate and productions. Zeniff also says, they multiplied and prospered in the land. In such a healthy country as Hassaurek describes, they would multiply: in such a fruitful country, they would prosper.

There is one noticeable feature in the record of the Nephites which strikes one who has lived only in our northern climate and zone: it is the rapidity with which they recovered from the disastrous effects of civil and religious commotions and bloody wars. The frequent allusions through the record to the wonderfully rapid prosperity which followed the cessation of strife is apt to strike the northern reader with surprise. But, when we become familiar with the character of the lands occupied by the Nephites, this surprise ceases. That which was known as the land of Nephi, comprehending an immense district of country, was so favored in climate and soil, was so abundantly blessed in all vegetables and minerals, and was generally so healthy that an industrious people like the Nephites would surround themselves with every comfort and luxury in, what would appear to the inhabitants of less favored localities, an incredibly short space of time.

The land settled by Nephi and his company had, without doubt, a healthy climate. We are not informed as to the age of Nephi or his brothers or their immediate descendants at their demise. But from the dates which are given, it is very evident they lived to a great age. Correct habits of living, with pure lives and the blessing of God upon them, promoted longevity. We think it is apparent from the record that, immediately after leaving Jerusalem, there was a remarkable increase in the duration of life among those who were called Nephites.

Jacob, who was born in the wilderness of Arabia, took charge of the plates after the death of his brother Nephi, and he bequeathed them to his son Enos. The year in which he gave them to Enos, in consequence of his own great age and approaching departure, is not given. Neither are we informed what the age of Enos was at the time he took possession of the plates. But Enos tells us that, one hundred and seventy-nine years from the time Lehi left Jerusalem, he himself began to be old and he saw that he must soon go down to the grave. How long he lived after this it is not stated; but from this date it is plain that Jacob and Enos must have lived to be very old men. Jacob was probably born soon after his parents left Jerusalem, so that his life and that of his son Enos must have nearly covered the period mentioned by the latter—one hundred and seventy-nine years.

The son of Enos and grandson of Jacob, whose name was Jarom, took charge of the plates after Enos. We do not know how old he was at the time they were handed to him; but we learn that he finished his writing upon them two hundred and thirty-eight years after Lehi left Jerusalem; that is, he had possession of the plates about fifty-nine years. From this it appears that he lived to be very old; for if Jacob, his grandfather, was born within four years after Lehi left Jerusalem, and Enos was born before Jacob was seventy-five years of age, Enos must have been at least one hundred years old at the time that he writes concering his approaching descent to the grave; and if Enos was born within seventy-nine years after Lehi left Jerusalem, and Jarom was born to Enos at the time the latter was fifty-nine years old, Jarom also must have been one hundred years old when he delivered the plates to his son Omni. If he lived to be one hundred years old, he must have been about forty-one years of age when his father delivered the records to him; but we are inclined to think he was older than this, and that his father Enos was at least one hundred and twenty years old when he died.

The plates containing the records were in the hands of Omni forty-four years, or until two hundred and eighty-two years from the departure of Lehi from Jerusalem. Thus we have four men in direct descent whose lives, from the birth of the first to the death of the fourth, cover a period of but little, if any, less than two hundred and eighty years! These are very remarkable instances of longevity. It speaks highly for the correctness of their habits and the salubriousness of the climate where they lived, and shows how greatly they were favored of the Lord.

Travelers inform us that in portions of the countries of Ecuador and Peru the inhabitants attain a very high age. In one valley in Ecuador visited by Hassaurek, the curate told him that persons who lived a hundred or more years did not at all constitute exceptional cases. Another traveler says:

"Longevity is common among the Peruvian Indians. I witnessed the burial of two, in a small village, one of whom had attained the age of one hundred and twenty-seven, and the other of one hundred and nine; yet both enjoyed unimpaired health to a few days before their decease. On examining the parish books of Barranca, I found, that in seven years, eleven Indians had been buried, whose joint ages amounted to one thousand two hundred and seven."

CHAPTER XIX.

TWO DISTINCT NATIONS—INTERMINGLED—MIXED BLOOD IN
LAMANITES—NEPHI AND COMPANY SETTLED IN AN
EARTHLY PARADISE—GREATLY PROSPERED—LAW OF
MOSES OBSERVED—A LIVE RELIGION—NEPHI CONVERSED
WITH THE SPIRIT OF THE LORD—HEARD VOICES OF THE
FATHER AND THE SON—UNDERSTOOD THE GOSPEL OF
JESUS—SIMPLICITY AND PLAINNESS OF HIS TEACHINGS,
PROPHECIES AND REVELATIONS—WONDERFUL EXTENT
AND VARIETY OF HIS KNOWLEDGE—WRITES OF THE
DAYS OF THE SAVIOR AS A CONTEMPORARY MIGHT—
EXACTNESS OF DESCRIPTION OF THE GREAT AND
ABOMINABLE CHURCH—ALSO THE EVENTS WHICH SHOULD
TAKE PLACE IN CONNECTION WITH ZION—ONLY TWO
CHURCHES—THE WHORE OF ALL THE EARTH SHOULD
GATHER MULTITUDES AMONG ALL THE NATIONS OF
GENTILES TO FIGHT AGAINST THE CHURCH OF THE
LAMB—POWER OF GOD POURED OUT UPON THE LATTER,
HIS WRATH UPON THE FORMER—THEY WHO FIGHT
AGAINST THE HOUSE OF ISRAEL SHALL WAR AMONG
THEMSELVES AND FALL INTO THE PIT THEY SHALL DIG
TO ENSNARE THE PEOPLE OF THE LORD—THE RIGHTEOUS
SHOULD NOT PERISH—GREAT VALUE OF THESE PRO-
MISES TO LATTER-DAY SAINTS—SECRET COMBINATIONS—
MANY CHURCHES TO BE BUILT UP—THEIR CHARACTER—THE
BOOK OF MORMON, HOW IT SHOULD BE RECEIVED—
CHURCHES PUT DOWN THE POWER AND MIRACLES OF
GOD—PREACH UP THEIR OWN WISDOM AND LEARNING—
CONTEND ONE WITH ANOTHER—GRIND THE POOR—
LITERAL FULFILLMENT AS LATTER-DAY SAINTS CAN
TESTIFY.

THE separation of Nephi and his people from Laman and
those who adhered to him made them a distinct nation.
Thus two nations—the Nephites and the Lamanites—grew up
upon this continent, as dissimilar and as much at variance in

their modes of thought and habits of life, in their religious
views and traditions and governmental policy and aims, as if
they were two races of widely separated and foreign origin.
Under the influence of two causes, which operated at different
periods almost through their entire existence, members of each
nation were led to intermingle and identify themselves with
the other; these were: apostacy from their religion on the part
of the Nephites, and conversion to its holy principles on the
part of the Lamanites. The Nephite nationality had an
existence of a little less than ten hundred years; but for nearly
the entire first six hundred of these, and a little more than the
last hundred, a wall of division existed between them and they
were distinct peoples. They had, however, mingled together
at various periods, as we have said, to such an extent that,
after the last great battle which resulted in the destruction of
the Nephite nationality, descendants of all the original families
were left among the survivors; so that the blood of Nephi, of
Sam, of Jacob, of Joseph and of Zoram still coursed in the
veins, as it does to this day, of those known by the name of
Lamanites; besides, there was the blood of the people known
as Zarahemlaites, who came to this land with Mulek, a son of
Zedekiah, king of Judah, and who were afterwards identified
with the Nephites.

The land to which Nephi and his company were led was
probably not excelled for fertility of soil, for healthfulness and
agreeableness of climate, for abundance and variety of vegetables
and minerals, for grandeur and beauty of scenery by any other
part of this "promised land" and certainly by no other land
outside of this continent. It abounded in all the elements
necessary to make a nation rich and powerful. It was an
earthly paradise. When they reached their new home they
devoted themselves to agriculture and the production of all
kinds of useful animals, as they had done when they first
landed on the continent. In these labors they were greatly
prospered, and they also multiplied rapidly. Their form of
religion was in strict conformity with the law of Moses. But
it was not with them a religion of empty forms and ceremonies.
Nephi had conversed in the wilderness, shortly after they had
left Jerusalem, with the Spirit of the Lord, as one man

speaketh to another; "for," said he, "I beheld he was in the form of a man; yet nevertheless I knew that it was the Spirit of the Lord." He had also heard the voices of both the Father and the Son. The Lord taught him heavenly things and led him by His voice from his boyhood all through his life. He understood the gospel of Jesus and taught it to his people in the greatest plainness, and without doubt administered unto them the ordinances thereof. His exposition of the first principles of the gospel, in the last three chapters of his second book (*II. Nephi, xxxi, xxxii and xxxiii chapters*) is as lucid and comprehensive as can be found in any of the divine records which have come to us. He informs us that he delighted and gloried in plainness, and certainly his prophecies and revelations which he recorded, and which are in the Book of Mormon, though they relate to stupendous and marvellous events, are conveyed in such simplicity and plainness that a child of ordinary understanding can comprehend the language. It is truly wonderful how exact and perfect his knowledge was concerning the name of the Savior, the name that His mother should bear, the time when and the place where He should be born, the events of His career, the doctrines which He should teach, the apostles whom He should select, the miracles which He should work, and the details of His persecution and death. Though he wrote but little short of 600 years before the Lamb of God appeared in the flesh, the incidents of His life are given with the minute fidelity of a well-informed contemporary.

It is not, however, his revelations concerning these which alone show the extent of his knowledge as a prophet of God. There is scarcely an event connected with our own day that he has not alluded to. A more graphic account than he gives of the condition of the people at the time the Book of Mormon should be revealed and come forth, and the effects which should follow its publication and the organization of the Church, is nowhere to be found. Indeed we do not see how a modern writer, familiar with all that has taken place in the time referred to, could in the same space, give a clearer description of these events than that given by Nephi in his record. This is due, of course, to the inspiration of the Lord which rested upon him. He saw by vision all these events take place as clearly as if he had been present in the flesh when they occurred.

He saw the Virgin Mary, the mother of the Son of God, and saw Him also as an infant and as a man; saw Him baptized by the prophet, and the Holy Ghost come down out of heaven upon Him; he saw Him go forth ministering unto the people, healing the sick, casting out devils and performing other mighty miracles, and he saw the twelve apostles following Him. He beheld the Lamb of God taken by the people and judged, lifted upon the cross and slain for the sins of the world; and afterwards saw the warfare that was waged against His apostles by the world. The Lord also revealed to him all that should take place upon this continent among his own descendants and the descendants of his wicked brethren; and he saw the Lamb of God descend from heaven and show Himself to those who should survive the terrible judgments which should take place at His crucifixion, and that He should also choose twelve apostles from among them to minister to them. The mighty events which should take place among them after this, up to the time the Nephite nation should be blotted out, as well as the fate which awaited the conquerors up to the discovery of the continent by white men; and afterwards until a remnant of them should receive the Book of Mormon which should be carried to them by believing Gentiles —Latter-day Saints, in fact—by means of which they should be brought to a knowledge of their ancestry and of the gospel which their fathers enjoyed; were all shown in vision to Nephi. He saw that the remnants of his and his brothers' descendants, known as Lamanites, would be killed a d driven and scattered by the white men who should cod e to this continent; but they should not all perish; the Lord would remember them, reveal His covenant to them, in which they should rejoice and many generations would not pass away among them until they should become a white and delightsome people. By vision, also, he saw that the Jews would be scattered among all nations; and that, at about the time the work of God would commence among the Lamanites, they would be gathered from the various nations and would return to their own land.

Like John, the beloved disciple, he has left on record his testimony concerning the great and abominable church, which should be among the Gentile nations. He saw that the devil was the foundation of that church. The desires of that great and abominable church were gold, silver, silks, scarlets, fine-twined linen, precious clothing and harlots; and that by it, for the praise of the world, the Saints of God would be destroyed and brought down into captivity. He saw that from the record of the Jews (the Bible) many parts which were plain and most precious and also many covenants of the Lord, all of which belonged to the gospel of the Lamb, were taken away by the great and abominable church, the object being to pervert the right ways of the Lord, that the eyes of the children of men might be blinded and their hearts be hardened. Because of this many of the Gentiles would stumble. Nephi calls that church, "the whore of all the earth;" she sat upon many waters and had dominion over all the earth, among all nations, kindreds, tongues and people.

He saw that after the Church of the Lamb would be organized there would be two churches only—the Church of the Lamb of God, and the church of the devil; whoso belongeth not to the former, belongeth to the other, the mother of abominations and the whore of all the earth. He saw that the numbers of the Church of the Lamb were few, because of the wickedness and abominations of the whore who sat upon many waters; and though they were also upon all the face of the earth, for the same reason that they were few in number, their dominions upon the face of the earth were small. Yet notwithstanding this was the condition of the Church of the Lamb, the mother of abominations was not satisfied. She wanted the Church of the Lamb destroyed. She gathered together multitudes upon the face of all the earth, among all the nations of the Gentiles, to fight against it.

How literally these predictions are being fulfilled in our day, upwards of fifty years after the publication of his record, and his record was published before there was any organization of the Church of the Lamb of God, we all know! But Nephi says (and it comes filled with consolation and encouragement to the Latter-day Saints) that he beheld the power of the Lamb

4*

of God upon the Saints of the Church of the Lamb and upon
the covenant people of the Lord, who were scattered upon all
the face of the earth, and they were armed with righteousness
and with the power of God in great glory. He beheld also
that the wrath of God was poured out upon the mother of
harlots, insomuch that there were wars and rumors of wars among
all the nations and kindreds of the earth. He was also told
that when this should take place. "at that day, the work
of the Father shall commence in preparing the way for the
fulfilling of His covenants which He had made to His people,
who are of the house of Israel." Nephi also predicted that
those who belonged to the great and abominable church should
war among themselves, and the sword of their own hands
should fall upon their own heads: and that every nation which
should war against the house of Israel should be turned one
against another, and they should fall into the pit which they
had dug to ensnare the people of the Lord. He said the
righteous should not perish, even if their enemies had to be
destroyed by fire; for the time must surely come that all they
who fight against Zion should be cut off. But he predicted the
overthrow and destruction of the churches which should belong
to the kingdom of the devil, the great whore of all the earth—
the churches which are built up to get gain, to get power over
the flesh, to become popular in the eyes of the world, which
seek the lusts of the flesh and the things of the world, and to
do all manner of iniquity; they had need to fear and tremble
and quake; they must be brought low in the dust; they must
be consumed as stubble.

The promises which the Lord made through Nephi in his
record are of the utmost value to the Church of Christ in our
day. How encouraging it is to know in the midst of the
deadly hostility against the work of God, and the incessant
attacks which are being made upon it that "he that fighteth
against Zion, both Jew and Gentile, both bond and free, both
male and female, shall perish!"

Nephi not only saw the emigration of the Gentile people to
this land, but he saw the struggle for independence and the results
which should follow. He described the growth of the nation,
the policy it should pursue towards the remnants of his own

and brothers' descendants, and the glorious destiny which it should achieve if it should espouse the gospel when it should be revealed; and, on the other hand, predicted the direful consequences which should follow its rejection by the nation.

Half a century and upwards has the rejection of the gospel, and a warfare against its believers now been continued, and we behold these direful consequences taking place, exactly as Nephi, inspired of God, said they should. The condition of the Gentile world at the time of the coming forth of the Book of Mormon and the organization of the Church in our day, is most accurately portrayed. Secret combinations should exist. Many churches would be built up; they would cause envyings, strifes and malice; and because of pride, of false teachers and false doctrines, their churches would become corrupted and lifted up. They would rob the poor, because of their fine sanctuaries; they would rob the poor, because of their fine clothing, and persecute the meek and poor, because in their pride they would be puffed up. Against the wise, and the learned, and the rich, that are puffed up in the pride of their hearts, and all those who preach false doctrines, and all those who commit whoredoms, and pervert the right way of the Lord, he says, the Lord has pronounced a wo, and said they should be thrust down to hell.

The very words which should be used, and which have been used, among the Gentile nations concerning the Book of Mormon after it should be published, are given by this great prophet; also the course which should be taken by the Gentiles who would believe and receive it, in carrying it to the present Indians—the descendants of himself and brothers—and the effect it would have upon them.

Though many churches would be built, they would put down the power and miracles of God, and preach up unto themselves their own wisdom and their own learning, that they might get gain and grind upon the face of the poor. One would say unto the other: "Behold I, I am the Lord's;" and the other would say: "I, I am the Lord's;" they would contend one with another; they would teach with their learning and deny the Holy Ghost which giveth the utterance. They would say, "Behold ye, hearken unto my precept; if they

shall say, there is a miracle wrought by the hand of the Lord,
believe it not; for this day He is not a God of miracles."

How completely and literally these predictions have been fulfilled, the Latter-day Saints, and especially the Elders who
have gone out to preach the gospel, can testify. They are eye
and ear witnesses to the truth of Nephi's record in the Book
of Mormon. The men who have opposed the work of God in
these days, have not thought that, in making use of the
expressions they have, they were fulfilling predictions recorded
in the Book of Mormon, and which were made upwards of
twenty-four hundred years ago. These words were published before the class had been tested by the Elders of the
Church of the Lamb, for at their publication the Church had
not been organized; but the Lord knew the language they
would use; He knew the spirit they would yield to; and He
inspired His servants to make the predictions. Had Nephi
been writing from personal experience with the class to which
he refers, he could not have quoted their stock phrases any
better. He has given us a picture, which possesses more than
photographic accuracy of detail, of society as it should exist
when the Book of Mormon should come forth, and the
changes which should take place subsequent to that event and
the organization of the Church, embracing also the fate that
will befall our own nation and the modern nations of Europe
under certain conditions which he specifies.

CHAPTER XX.

NEPHI'S COMMANDMENT TO JACOB CONCERNING SMALL
PLATES—NEPHI ANOINTS A MAN TO BE KING—HIS SUC-
CESSORS IN KINGLY DIGNITY CALLED BY HIS NAME—
PATRIARCHAL GOVERNMENT—JACOB PRESIDED OVER
THE CHURCH—KING MOSIAH'S MODE OF LIFE—SEERS AS
WELL AS KINGS—WAS THERE A CHANGE OF DYNASTY?
—KINGLY AND PRIESTLY AUTHORITY UNITED IN MOSIAH.

FIFTY-FIVE years from the time that Lehi left Jerusalem,
Nephi gave a commandment to his brother Jacob concerning the small plates upon which he had engraved so many
revelations and so much doctrine. He desired his brother to
keep them and to hand them down to his children after him ;
and to be sure and pursue the same course with them that he
had—engrave upon them sacred things which were preached
and any great revelations or prophecies that might be given.
Jacob did this ; and they remained in the hands of his lineage
until Amaleki, who was a descendant of his, placed them in
the custody of King Benjamin. Jacob does not inform us, in
his book that we have received, how long this was before the
death of Nephi ; but, as he says in the same connection, that
Nephi began to be old, and saw that he must die, it is probable that it was only a short time.

It was then that Nephi anointed a man to be a king and a
ruler over his people. He was so greatly beloved by them,
through his self-sacrificing and continuous labors for them and
his courage in defending them ; (for he had been compelled to
have recourse to the sword of Laban, and to wield it in their
defense against the attacks of the Lamanites) ; that they were
desirous to retain in remembrance his name. They, therefore,
called his successors Second Nephi, Third Nephi, etc., "let
them be of whatever name they would."

The government was, without doubt, more patriarchal than
monarchical in its character. Upon one occasion, Nephi's

brother, Jacob, in addressing the people, uses this language: "Having been called of God, and ordained after the manner of His holy order, and having been consecrated by my brother, Nephi, *unto whom ye look as a king or a protector, and on whom ye depend for safety.*" Yet Nephi himself informs us that his people desired that he should be their king; "but," he adds, "I, Nephi was desirous that they should have no king; nevertheless, I did for them according to that which was in my power." This explains the relationship which he bore to them. He taught them the will of God, administered ordinances unto them, was their leader in all civil and religious matters in repelling the attacks of their enemies and was able to teach them mechanism and the arts of manufacturing. To such a man his people would naturally look, as Jacob says, as a king or protector. Before his death, it appears that he chose his brother, Jacob—who was a man of great faith and a prophet, and who, with Joseph, another brother, had been ordained a priest and teacher by him over the land of the Nephites—to take the lead in all spiritual matters and to have charge of the records upon which the more sacred things were to be kept, and anointed another to be ruler in civil affairs. Whether it was one of his own sons or not, we are not informed, neither is it stated that this office was made hereditary. From what is said subsequently in the record respecting the kings, however, it seems clear that this office did descend from father to son; but the people also had a voice in choosing the king. The brief allusion which is made to these kings by Jarom nearly two centuries after Nephi's death, shows that for that period they had been mighty and faithful men of God. Upwards of four hundred years after Nephi's departure, a glimpse is given us of the mode of life which the king led. Speaking of Mosiah, son of Benjamin, it is said, "And King Mosiah did cause his people that they should till the earth. And he also, himself, did till the earth, that thereby he might do according to that which his father had done in all things."

Such a monarchy as is here described, would be an inexpensive form of government, and it is probable that it was chiefly of this character from the beginning. We know that the two kings who preceded Mosiah were like himself—prophets of God. He, himself, was a seer, also, as was his grandfather of the same name, and most likely his father, Benjamin; and he had in his possession the Urim and Thummim. Such men ruled the people in righteousness and as kind fathers, and kept the expense of government down to the lowest point. Whether or not there was a change of dynasty when the first Mosiah was chosen king, is not cartain from what is written by Amaleki in the Book of Omni, though it does not appear improbable. Neither does it appear why the kings, Mosiah, Benjamin and Mosiah, were not called by the dynastic name of Nephi, according to the custom which prevailed during the long lifetime of Jacob, and probably afterwards. If a change of dynasty did occur, this custom may have been changed, though scarcely for that cause alone, as Nephi was still the reveared founder of the nation; it may be that the dynastic name was omitted, and their own names mentioned, for the purpose of better distinguishing them. When the record which was kept by the kings upon the other plates of Nephi shall be brought forth, we shall have knowledge respecting the history of the Nephites, covering this period of upwards of four centuries, that will be of inestimable value. One thing, however, is plain from that which has come to us, that when the first Mosiah became king, in him was again united the kingly and priestly authority.

CHAPTER XXI.

NEPHI DIED—EXAMPLE OF HIS LIFE—INTERNAL EVIDENCE
OF DIVINITY OF HIS WRITINGS IN THE SPIRIT OF GOD
WHICH ACCOMPANIES THEM—AN EVENTFUL CAREER—
ADMIRABLE IN EVERY RELATION—A BORN LEADER,
SUCCESSFUL AS A MECHANIC, MINER, SEAMAN, CHEMIST,
METALLURGIST, STOCK-RAISER, AGRICULTURIST, MANU-
FACTURER AND STATESMAN—EXPANDED VIEWS OF THE
RIGHTS AND EQUALITY OF MAN—RELIGIOUS LIBERTY—
THE END.

"AND it came to pass that Nephi died." In this simple
language does Jacob record this event. He leaves
Nephi's works to speak for him. And their consideration cannot fail to be of profit to all who will give them attention.
The example of such a life is of immense benefit to mankind;
it strengthens, elevates and inspires with noble purpose all who
become acquainted with it. No Latter-day Saint can read the
life of Nephi, as he has given it to us in his record, without
being incited to exersise greater faith, to live nearer to God
and to cherish loftier aims.

It can be said about the writings of Nephi (and this is also
true of the entire Book of Mormon, and in fact of all saving
truth) that they bring the conviction of their divinity to the
heart of every one who reads them in the spirit in which they
are written. Read in that spirit, they fill the soul with a sweet
and heavenly joy that only the Spirit of God can produce.

The career of Nephi was a most eventful one. He passed
through many trials and afflictions; he was often in positions
of peril: but he never yielded, never faltered, nor never shrunk
from any ordeal to which he was exposed. In every relation
of life he admirably performed his part. As a son, he was all
his father could desire, and of this Lehi bore ample testimony
before he died. As a brother he did all in his power to benefit
and save his kindred. What his course was with those who

followed and cast their lots with him, we can understand by reading his teachings, his labors and the love in which they held him while living and his memory when dead. He was patient, persevering, energetic and skillful ; a man who was evidently born to lead. He exhibited these qualities. when required to return to Jerusalem. Afterwards in the wilderness it seemed as though the company would all have perished had it not been for his good sense and capacity as a hunter. In building the ship, in its management upon the ocean, in teaching his people to work in wood and in metals of all kinds—iron, copper, brass, steel, silver, and gold—he exhibited his skill as a mechanic, a miner, a seaman, chemist and metallurgist. He manufactured swords and other weapons of defense, he built houses, he cultivated the ground, he raised flocks and herds, he built a temple, which though not so costly as Solomon's, was constructed after its pattern, and the workmanship upon it was exceedingly fine; he taught his people to be skillful, industrious and how to apply their labor to the best advantage; as a statesman he organized society upon a firm and permanent basis, laid the foundation of civil and religious liberty; gave shape to the government and polity and implanted in the breasts of his people such a love for and a determination to maintain equal rights that the effects were felt, it may be said in truth, through all the generations of his race. Understanding as he did the government of the Lord, before whom there are no privileged classes, he respected the rights of the people; and while he knew there must be officers to bear responsibility and a properly organized government, he knew also that it should be based upon the consent of the people. He brought with him to this "promised land" the broadest conceptions respecting the principle of human equality and the rights of men. Some of his views we gather from his teachings. Speaking of the Lord, he says: "And He inviteth them all to come unto Him and partake of His goodness; and He denieth none that come unto Him, black and white, bond and free, male and female; and He remembereth the heathen, and all are alike unto God, both Jew and Gentile." The nobility in which he evidently believed, was the nobility of good deeds. The perfect performance of duty would ennoble the poorest and the lowliest

and make him the peer of the richest and the best born.
While his people were true to his teachings, this sentiment
always prevailed.   They enjoyed the largest liberty consistent
with the preservation of good order.   Every man had the
greatest freedom of belief.   Theft, robbery, violence, adultery
and murder were all punished under the law; but there was no
law against a man's belief; persecution of religion, however
erroneous or false the religion might be, was expressly forbid-
den and was made punishable.   In this way the equality and
free agency of the people were preserved, and they were left
at liberty to choose for themselves their faith and form of worship.   So far as his influence and teachings went among the
people, they were free and the country was a land of liberty
unto them.

We here close the life of Nephi.   He has shown us how
much a mortal man, who devotes himself to God and His work,
can accomplish for himself and his fellow-mortals, and how
near, by the exercise of faith, man can draw to God.